HEATH

ADDISON JAMES

ADDISON JAMES

For B: The best friend anyone could ask for, the best sister in the universe, and my first ever reader. Thank you for always listening—nothing would have ever happened without your support.

CONTENTS

A Note From The Author

Heath takes place about four centuries before the events of Callum and is about the early days of Heath and Chase's relationship.

Each book can be read as a standalone, and each book has a happily ever after for the couple it is about. However, if you want to know about the larger world of the Crae siblings, I hope I do a satisfactory job of exploring it here.

A note about the word: in this world, all characters who have fated mates have no idea who they'll end up with. This resulted in me envisioning a world where everyone is bisexual, which felt nice as a queer author.

CONTENT NOTES

- MMC is the secret/unacknowledged child

- War

- Imprisonment/solitary confinement/mental stress and harm due to imprisonment (with the MMC and others)

- Fighting, including killing enemies

- Eye trauma (permanent)

- Learning to adapt to permanent injury

Chapter One

Chase

"What I really need is for one of you cowards to stand up and be willing to handle my son."

King Galaus, unrightful ruler of Demonheim, feared among all who know his name, snarls the words at the circle of us gathered in his gaudy throne room. It's supposed to sound menacing, I suppose, but all I can think is that if he wants Ryder dead, then he should be willing to do it himself.

It's the vitriol that he uses to spit the word *son*. He has to be delusional to expect that line to land in this room.

At least five of us here are his sons. We're the unacknowledged sons, the ones who mean nothing to his precious family line. The ones he had before he stole a throne, and the ones who are therefore not a danger to him and his future.

We're the usable sons. The ones meant to be so desperate that we'll go and kill the rightful king of Demonheim for him.

I look around the room as subtly as I can. The worst part is the grandeur and menace have done their job. Almost everyone looks, if not enthusiastic, then at least like his words are worth listening to.

It's that damned sword, I think. It's convinced everyone that he belongs here, when that couldn't be further from the truth.

Well, it's that sword and whatever power he's managed to claw out of the realm. He might not be the rightful ruler of Demonheim, but he can act like it well enough.

He relies heavily on the image of menace and power that the sword lends him, even going so far as to use the human concept of hell to inspire his vision of the realm. With floors and walls of obsidian black, the stone so stark and deep it reminds me of an endless void, this room would already be unsettling before one considers the lines of red-hot magma shooting through the floor.

It should make him look like someone pretending to have power, but the violently glinting sword leaning next to his burnished gold throne quells all mocking.

I can't take my eyes off the sword. Most of us try not to look at it, try not to consider it. Most of the time, we fail. It's hard to forget an object capable of so much destruction.

"Begging your pardon, your majesty," one of my father's loyal advisors simpers, "But I do think our first issue needs to be the waves of demons escaping the realm, and dealing with whoever is helping them leave."

I fight to keep a neutral face while they talk about hunting me down right to my face.

"Demons leaving is an abomination," my father agrees. "A betrayal. Treason of the highest order."

Truthfully, demons leaving the realm weakens the magic of the realm and therefore weakens the ruler. It's one of the reasons why I've helped so many escape.

"It takes quite a bit of magic to open a portal," the king muses. "Who would have that magic?"

There are some uneasy looks from people in this room, and I fight to keep my gaze forward and only loosely focused, lest anyone look at me too long.

Not that anyone would assume I am the culprit. It does take quite a bit of magic, but Demonheim has always liked me, and the magic cooperates with me. I understand the realm and its rules, and I can navigate my way around them easily enough.

I've been able to slip past everyone unnoticed for years now. I'm an unremarkable son of my father's and always have been. I'm no great fighter, or scholar, or courtier. By all appearances, I'm a rather average son, given a position simply by virtue of being a bastard-born son and therefore worthy of being watched.

Or at least, so they think.

The king snaps, drawing all our attention immediately. People die when he feels ignored, and we've all long ago learned to be on our toes around him. "I want a list of whoever might possess that level of magic," he says. "I want it as soon as possible. I also want three viable plans of attack to take out my son before he truly does irreversible damage to the realm. Do you understand?"

We all chorus our agreement, capable of saying nothing else. Fariq, one of my father's most loyal advisors—and likely his oldest son, although none of us would discuss that openly—takes charge and divides the group. "You four, you're with me to plan an attack. You four, have those names together within a fortnight."

Well, at least I don't have to plan an attack on Ryder. I just have to do whatever it takes to keep my own name off the list I've been assigned to compile.

***

We agree to bring preliminary lists together for the next day, and then I turn around and make my way to a secret room near the libraries.

Demonheim is a realm for demons, made with demon magic, and it always gives to those it likes. I don't know if Demonheim likes me or if it likes the rebellion, but either way, it always makes space for us to meet.

The door opens for me with a soft pulse of magic, and I close it quickly behind me, adjusting to the dim light of the room.

Inside wait two families, each with young demons. I always feel particularly bad for the families, for the mothers who don't want their children to grow up in a place like this.

Who knows, if my own mother thought that my father was bad news, maybe none of us would be in this position now.

"Ready to go?"

"Is it safe now?" One of the fathers asks, looking around furtively like someone might jump out of the shadows.

"Is anything ever safe?" I retort, then take a deep breath. "Safe enough. Let's go."

Sneaking through the halls of Demonheim undetected is no easy feat. Even if the realm likes us, even if it does everything it can to assist us, the fact remains that Demonheim is home to thousands of demons, and anyone might stumble on us at any moment.

Still, the portal only opens in one location. I tried to get the realm to open it somewhere more convenient, and I passed out for two days from trying to channel that amount of magic. There doesn't seem to be a way around traipsing through the entire realm, no matter how dangerous it might be.

So I bring the families to the portal, located at the back of a quiet garden. It's closed now, but just a touch from me will open it.

"Go quickly," I murmur, laying my hand on the stonework to open the way for them.

The second family is only halfway through when I hear a shout behind me. I whirl quickly to see two enterprising young soldiers rushing for the portal, swords drawn.

"Go," I snap at the father still near me, mind already spinning, trying to determine how best to handle this.

I'm not sure I could kill the soldiers on my own, and that seems like the only option to keep them quiet. Taking a risk, I step through the portal, following the family to the other side.

The world I emerge in is much greener than Demonheim. It's much louder than where the portal was as well. The families I brought over are running now, ducking behind Hannah and the soldiers she's acquired for her and her mate's coup.

Hannah's eyes go wide at the sight of me, but before she can do anything, soldiers spill out behind me. It's not just the two I saw, either. It's more than a dozen, all of them with weapons drawn, charging into the fray.

They're met with steel, and I have to side-step a blade coming at me. It's from one of Hannah's soldiers, but most of them don't know me at all, and don't know that I'm on their side.

It's probably for the best, I think, doing everything I can to block and not attack. I'm not quite the swordsman he is, and just when I'm debating if I dare risk doing magic after already opening the portal, Hannah smoothly steps in, pushing her soldier out of the way.

"The portal is compromised," I tell her, stating the obvious. "I don't know how to get anyone else out."

We always knew the portal was risky, but getting demons out of Demonheim was the only aspect of this rebellion that was actually working.

She's bizarrely calm as she nods. "We have a plan," she says. "Look for a wolf. He'll help us end this."

The fighting quiets around us, and I realize that the demons who followed me through are dead.

Hannah drops her weapon but doesn't sheathe it. "Go back," she says. "Tell them you escaped. But wait for our wolf. He'll need you to be his guide."

I want to ask for more, but there's no time. I just nod, then dart back through the portal, letting it close once I make it through.

I sway on my feet as the magic leaves me, the cost of bending the rules of time and space like that sapping my strength.

But I can't let that show. There's a dozen more guards watching me, and I need to have a story ready for them.

Chapter Two

Heath

I 've been in plenty of war camps in my life, but I've never been in one with quite so many refugees.

The camp has more displaced people than it does soldiers. I can't walk through the place without almost tripping on a dozen children running about.

If this is the last great hope for Demonheim, then maybe I should already give up the place as lost. But then again, Celia has told me a thousand times that I've always been stubborn.

I finally get to the center of the camp, the only part that still looks like they're actively preparing for war, and not simply the remnants of a war already lost.

A tall demon greets me at the flap of a large war tent. "You came," she says.

I raise an eyebrow, looking her up and down. "I did. You look..."

She tosses her hair over her shoulder, which only shows me the mottled bruising covering her face and neck. It also highlights the delicate points of her ears and her small black horns.

"Don't worry about it," she says simply. "The latest batch of refugees were followed through the portal. I took care of the problem."

She's alive, and I don't have to ask to know that whoever she faced is not. I've never seen Hannah give someone a second chance to hurt her.

The bruises must be fresh, barely an hour or so old, if they are still this vivid. "I'm sorry I didn't get here sooner."

"I didn't ask for your assistance in small battles," she says, stepping aside. "Come in."

The tent is well appointed but not grand. While the canvas walls of the tent might make it look like a temporary structure, the furniture inside is all more permanent, with a wooden bed on one side and a large desk on the other.

Sitting behind the desk is another demon, and I know without asking who he is. The rightful king, the heir to Demonheim. Ryder, king of the demons.

He stands when I enter. "Prince Heath."

"Just Heath."

"Then I'm Ryder." He gestures to the other chair across his desk, then sits again. "I'm pleased you've come."

I look him over. His hair is shorn close to the scalp, making his horns stand out all the more obviously. They're larger than Hannah's and indeed larger than any other demon's I've met. Perhaps it's the crown of the true king.

Even with those horns, he looks young. He looks too young for people to be following him to war, even though I know very well that looks can be deceiving for people like us.

"I told Hannah I would." I look at her sidelong, but she looks straight ahead, not looking away from her mate.

Ryder is looking at her too, naked adoration on his face.

I clear my throat, hoping to dispel the look. I get enough of that at home, between my sister and her mate. I don't need it during what might turn into a war.

"It's in the wolves' best interests to have stable leadership in Demonheim," I tell him. "So I'm here. Where can I best serve?"

It is in the wolves' best interest, and I wish I could have made Celia see that before I left. But in reality, it's more than that.

I'm here because this is my fault, and I want to see it made right.

"I'm tired of just barely saving refugees," Ryder says, staring intently at Hannah's bruises. "We shouldn't be fleeing the kingdom."

I agree. This isn't how you win a war. This is just how you ensure the loss is slow and drawn out.

"Hannah says you have a reputation for this sort of thing."

"What sort of thing?" I ask, applying a careful mask of politeness. I've spent my life as both a royal and a soldier, and I've learned that often the two cannot cross. That when I'm a prince of the werewolves, there's a certain polite game we all play, a fiction that the ugly things we all do don't exist. But when I'm a soldier, I am someone entirely different.

Hannah doesn't seem to have time for that game, though. "The sort of thing that can cause the direction of power to change hands permanently."

I consider the statement. While technically correct, I think she gives me more credit than I deserve.

I'm not a master strategist. I'm just very good at being in the right place at the right time. My mother used to say I was always too clever by half, and better at getting myself into and out of trouble than anyone she'd ever met.

Perhaps that's all Hannah and Ryder need from me.

"I'll do it." I don't need to think about it. I've already thought about it for weeks, weighing my options. My sister doesn't want me here, doesn't think this is our fight. But I'm half to blame for this, so I've long since made up my mind about what I need to do.

***

My new allies want to talk me through every inch of their war, their plan, and their camp, but I barely listen. Talk. It's always too much talk.

Celia and Bryce have always been about the talk, Celia more reluctantly than Bryce. But I was relieved when Callum came along fifty years later. Finally, someone who understood the importance of action.

I'm craving action here. Now that I've entered this fight, I'd like to get into it. Like to finish it, if I can.

And there's only one way to do that.

I interrupt Ryder's prattling on about the refugees emerging day after day. "What I really need to know about," I tell him, "is Demonheim itself. The physical layout."

"That's going to be hard," he says. "Demonheim is not stable, like a castle or a town. It's shifting based on demons and their needs. Demon magic helps grasp it, but I can't give you that. It's something you have or you don't."

"We thought of that," Hannah interrupts smoothly. "We have a contact for you. Once you find him, he can guide you through." She touches the bruises on her face. "I spoke to him this morning. He's waiting for you."

"Who am I looking for?"

"My brother," Ryder says. "Half brother. He's still there. He's been helping refugees slip out, and he'll help you."

"I wasn't aware you had any siblings."

"I have plenty, I think. My father never saw a need to limit himself. In all fairness, Chase is quite a bit older than me, so my father wasn't with my mother yet."

"And he'll help?" I ask, ignoring the family politics of the demon king.

"Chase is loyal," Hannah says firmly. "He'll help."

"If I can't navigate my way through Demonheim, how do I find him?"

"If you're lucky, he'll find you."

That's not especially reassuring, but I nod. I've done more with less.

The mission is relatively simple. Get into the highly guarded realm. Sneak through an unnavigable maze. If I'm lucky, meet up with a spy I've never met and have no strong way of identifying. And then commit a murder against an incredibly powerful king, in possession of an unmentionably powerful magical artifact.

No wonder Celia cursed me out when I told her I was leaving.

"Any questions?" Ryder asks me.

A thousand, most likely. But only one he can actually answer. "Tell me about the sword."

Hannah bares her teeth at just the thought of it. "You know about the sword."

Hannah's right. She and I were the ones who found it and brought it to Demonheim.

I'd owed her a favor. Hannah had saved my life in our last battle together, and when she'd been given an impossible bounty, I'd agreed to help. We'd recovered the sword together.

And accidentally set off this awful chain of events, leading us to where we are now.

So really, no matter how much Celia curses at me and forbids me from getting involved in things outside of our pack, I know I need to be here. I owe it to them.

"Tell me more. Tell me about what he's done with it, since he stole it from his wife."

Hannah huffs. "He wields it without restraint. At this point he doesn't actually need to lift it much; everyone is more than aware of what it can do."

Most immortals can only be killed by catastrophic incidents. Burning so hot and fast our healing cannot keep up, taking out the entire body at once, is one way to do it. The other is separating the head completely from the neck.

That sword might as well make us all mortal. Wounds from the sword don't heal. In that one place, our immortality is gone forever.

It's no wonder King Galaus has used it to strike fear into the hearts of the demons.

"Where does he keep it?"

"Right next to him. At all times," Ryder says heavily, his shoulders tensing at the thought. "I presume it's taken my mother's place in their bed, frankly."

"Your mother?"

"Missing. Presumed dead. You didn't know?"

"I thought she'd fled with you." I hadn't thought about her at all, I realize with a sinking feeling.

I hadn't had the best opinion of her; she'd made things difficult for Hannah when she was younger, and I'd heard all about it. The queen might not have been outright cruel, but she'd never helped Hannah when other demons cast her aside. But to be murdered by her spouse is a fate I wouldn't wish on anyone.

Ryder takes a moment to gather himself, but nods. "At any rate, the sword never leaves his side. That's the problem."

"That makes it harder," I muse, already thinking through options.

Hannah raises her eyebrow. "That's why I asked for you."

It's probably meant to be flattering, but flattery won't solve the problem in front of me.

Still. I know what I agreed to. I force a smile onto my face. "When do we start?"

Chapter Three

Heath

Hannah walks me to the portal alone after Ryder promises her with a kiss to have it opened and ready for us.

"So, queen of the demons," I say, smirking at her. "Is it what you wanted?"

Hannah, who always just wanted demons to *like* her, to accept her even with her pointed ears and weak demon magic, will now rule them all. It's a reversal of fates that I don't think anyone could have predicted.

"I still feel more like a mercenary than a queen," she says. "What about this is different to any war camp we were in?"

It's true. "And after?" I press. "Will you be satisfied when this is over?"

She sighs. "Ask me when it's over. That doesn't feel real, yet. But I do know that for Ryder, I'll do whatever it takes."

Mating bonds. I suppose if my sister could crawl back from her grief for Bethany, then Hannah agreeing to sit on a throne beside the boy-king isn't too surprising.

"And besides, I think if anyone could truly change Demonheim, it'll be Ryder. You don't know him, Heath, but if you did... demons aren't known for our idealism, but there's something good about him."

I bite back the first comments that come to mind, because they're not fair. Demons aren't inherently cruel or bad. Just because Demonheim holds the darkest among us, just because demon magic can be used to ensnare the unaware, doesn't mean they're evil.

But calling the future king of demon-kind good, like he has some special type of purity, seems a little ridiculous. Kings can't be all good, and kings at war certainly can't.

But that's not my place to say. "I'm happy you're happy, Hannah," I tell her. "And I'll do what I can to make that future possible for you."

"I know," she says. "I told Ryder you were the one to ask. You've always had a talent for this type of thing, Heath."

A soft glowing of the mist on the horizon tells me we're reaching the portal entrance. It must take an uncommon amount of magic to maintain it, and I shudder to think of the king who powers it remotely, casually, like it's nothing to use this much power.

She stops. "This is where I leave you. Good luck, Heath."

I turn to her. "Any last words of wisdom?"

"Keep your weapons close. Don't trust anyone but Chase. And Heath—please." She stops, like she can't quite think of what she wants to say, but that's fine. I understand, anyway.

We've never been ones for sentimentality. We watched each other's backs in tenuous situations, and then never acknowledged it again. But now, there's a glow to her eyes, and I turn away before I have to acknowledge it.

I absently check for my weapons one last time and then walk into the mist.

***

The mist goes on for so long that it takes me a minute to process the change in smell. I've arrived on the other side, then, but Demonheim is exactly as tricky and unnavigable as Ryder and Hannah both warned.

The fog is even thicker here, like the realm itself is trying to stymie my progress. Fucking demon magic, inscrutable and complicated and fucking irritating.

All magic is irritating, but demon magic is a special brand, relying on complicated deals and clauses, always unapproachable to outsiders, which is clearly evident by the very realm fighting to keep me out.

I suppose it's a defense mechanism. Demonheim is, after all, designed as a sort of prison, a place to keep the very worst of us, the ones we choose not to kill for whatever reason. Demons are gods-designed to be the jailors, and it makes sense for a jail to be unnavigable by everyone but the jailors.

The gods think of everything, I suppose. Except for the fact that I am a wolf, and they can design this land however they want. My senses won't lie to me.

So I close my eyes and ignore all the extraneous stimuli, taking a deep breath.

My eyes shoot open.

I didn't expect to scent anything in particular; I just wanted to determine a way forward. But the minute I open my wolf senses fully, I find the sweetest, most alluring scent I've ever smelled in my life.

Like the spiced apple cider Bethany makes in the autumn, only a thousand times more potent. I've never scented anything like it before, but the wolf in me knows what I'm scenting before my mind can even process it.

Mate.

I close my eyes again, taking off through the mist at a run.

Chapter Four

Chase

I've gone over the story a thousand times in my head before I even make it to another demon that I need to say it out loud to. It's a good thing, too, because Fariq's questioning is intense.

I was on a walk. No, not going anywhere in particular. I saw them escaping through a portal. I think it was opened by the father of the second family. I charged in after them, and several others followed me. I am the only survivor.

I feel bad for using that poor father's name, for blaming this on him, but if all goes well, he won't be back in Demonheim until my father is gone.

Fariq isn't stupid. No one that is close to the king is stupid, and there are too many reasons to doubt my story. After all, they all know I'm only moderately accomplished as a fighter. There's a reason I wasn't chosen for the team planning to lead a war party to kill Ryder. So believing that I was the sole survivor in an attack against Hannah and Ryder's forces would be a stretch for anyone.

I thought of this on the way to the war room we're currently planning in. The easiest way to turn suspicion from me is to point out some of the things I've noticed about their war camp. I didn't see much, but some secrets might make things easier for me.

It's a gamble, but it's not like I was left in a good position. Hannah and Ryder can just learn to live with it.

"Again."

I sigh. Fariq has made me tell the story a dozen times, like the details will suddenly change. But I've rehearsed too much for that.

As stories go, I think I concocted a good one. And I'll tell it a million times if that's what it takes.

The story is practically rote now, so I let my mind drift, thinking of what Hannah told me on the other side of the portal.

A wolf. There's a wolf coming, and he's supposedly going to save us all.

What a wolf can do that a demon can't, I don't know. But if he really can end this, then I'll do whatever it takes.

"We should have you tell the king what you saw—" Fariq begins.

There's a strange rush of magic, a prickling like static, and it makes all my hair stand on end. I look around surreptitiously, but no one else seems to have noticed.

It's Demonheim, speaking directly to me, the magic of the realm getting my attention.

And that can only mean one thing.

"You should tell the king," I interrupt him. "He wants to hear from you more than me, and you know the story well enough." I stand, trying to make myself look like I'm not in a rush, even though I absolutely am. "And I have a list to compile, anyways."

"We know which demon opened the portal now," he says, exasperation evident as he moves to block me from the exit.

I dodge around him. I don't want to look like I'm desperate to leave, but it can't be helped, I suppose. "We don't know that he's the only one."

And then I'm out the door and doing my best to not break into a run.

Something is waiting for me, and I'm desperate to find out what it is.

CHAPTER FIVE

HEATH

The scent grows sharper, so I assume I'm getting closer. *My mate, my mate, my mate.* The thought consumes me entirely. I can't think of Hannah, or Ryder, or the struggle for the sovereignty of Demonheim. All I know is what's in front of me, where I must go.

Mate.

I've waited nearly six centuries for my mate. If they're here, now, if the waiting is finally over—

The air changes, and I dare to open my eyes to see where I am in this labyrinthian realm. The mist has weakened, revealing to me a scene that makes my heart thump loud enough I'm surprised I'm not immediately noticed.

I'm in a hallway, dark stone seemingly entombing me here, the narrow hallway forcing travel in one direction. But that's okay, because standing at the end is the most beautiful man I've ever seen.

This must be my mate. This man, this beautiful man—sandy hair, obsidian demon horns poking out of his loose curls, and eyes so wide and deep when he sees me. He's my mate, and I can feel it in my bones, like something snapping into place. Like the whole world is sharper, brighter, now that he's here in front of me.

I stop moving, my muscles refusing to work. I want nothing more than to go to him, to wrap him in my arms, to fall to my knees in front of him, but he's completely still with his surprise, and I don't want to startle him further.

His eyes trail over me, moving too fast. "You're Hannah's contact?" He looks around surreptitiously, like he's waiting for enemies to jump out from the shadows. For all I know, that could be an actual concern here.

I want to tell him yes. I want to tell him what I'm doing here, that I've come to help. But what comes out is only, "You're my mate."

It's not surprising, perhaps, considering the wolf in me. We're always going to think about our mates before anyone or anything else; we can't be blamed for our single-minded devotion. But it doesn't seem to soothe my mate.

His frantic staring grows somehow more desperate. "Here?" he rasps. I'm not sure exactly what he's reacting to, so I just watch. "Now?"

"Here," I agree. "Now." I step forward, drawn to him. "I'm Heath."

"Chase," he says, stepping closer as if he too can't resist. "Can I—"

I don't know what he's asking for, so I wait for him to elaborate. "Demons don't know our mates on sight," he mutters, and I don't bother to correct that sight has nothing to do with it. For a wolf, everything is about scent. His smell is divine and I desperately ache for more of it.

"We need touch," he continues. "So, can I..."

I nod eagerly, walking over to him. I must look like a desperate child, but I couldn't care less. This is my mate. If he wants to touch me, then I would walk through fire to let him.

His hand lands on mine, a gentle, tentative touch. The touch is barely there, scarcely a brush. And I'm not some green young thing, so a single touch should not make me feel better than anything in the past ever has. And yet it's a shock to my body, an overwhelming feeling like my heart has stopped and restarted just for this one man.

Chase's eyes are closed in what looks like rapture. "Chase?" I murmur, turning my hand under his so I can stoke his fingers.

He shudders like I grabbed his cock. "Gods, that is something," he murmurs.

"What is it?" I ask, because touching my mate feels like a divine revelation, but Chase is very clearly feeling something physical right now.

"Mates, the energy..." he shakes his head. "You wouldn't understand, but it's a purer form of energy. Purer than any other demon bargain. And I've heard about it, but..." He shakes his head again. "I get it now."

He's right, I don't understand, but I'm irrationally pleased that I'm already able to make my mate feel good, and I haven't even shown him what I can do with my tongue yet.

I lean in closer and take a long draw of Chase's scent, letting it fill every inch of me.

I owe my sister an apology for every time I criticized her for being distracted by her mate. This is like an impossible loop, his scent drawing me in further and further, blinding me to everything else.

But then a nagging thought forces its way in, reminding me of where we are. This is not the place to fall into my mate like this. I step back, forcing myself to focus so I can survey my surroundings.

This hallway is too exposed, and simultaneously too enclosed. Anyone could come upon us, and we'd have no chance of escape.

Chase, seemingly, has the same thought. "Some of the king's advisors are right through that door," he mutters. "So unless you want to start this fight now, we need to move."

"Do you have somewhere we can go?" I ask. I'm slightly ashamed to admit that only half my mind is on planning for war.

"Yes. We'll be—well, it's as safe as anywhere else is around here."

And that's all I can ask for, really. So I nod, taking his hand again, some instinct driving me, as if he's going to walk away and leave me here. And I can't have that.

And if I get to see the slack-jawed look on his face when our skin touches again? Then that's just another incentive to not stop touching him.

"I don't know how to get anywhere else," I manage to explain, tearing my eyes from his face to make myself think more clearly. "So you have to lead the way."

I can feel him staring at me, can smell his scent shifting, growing somehow even sweeter. "Chase?" I prompt, voice a little breathier than I'd like.

He forcibly turns away from me, although I note with pride that he doesn't drop my hand. "Alright," he rasps, and then turns his attention rather resolutely to the wall to our left.

Only it's not a wall anymore. It's a corridor, and I do my best not to gape at it. "If I fucking knew how to do that..." I mutter.

Chase doesn't acknowledge that, just grips my hand tighter and pulls me down the corridor.

CHAPTER SIX

CHASE

Demonheim responds to my needs, as it always does, showing the way to my rooms. They're simple, with just a bedroom and a small sitting area, but they're mine.

That's one of the beautiful parts of Demonheim. No one else should be able to get into these rooms.

Well, no one but me and this wolf. The one who's following me with a grip on my hand like he's afraid I'll disappear in a puff of smoke.

Heath. Hannah and Ryder's chosen savior, the one who's supposed to help me take back this realm. The one I've been waiting for, the one who will supposedly make taking down the king possible.

My mate. One touch from him was all it took to confirm it; the energy from him is so strong it's nearly bowling me over. It's pure in a way nothing I've ever felt before is.

My door swings open without me needing to touch it, and I squeeze Heath's hand to guide him inside, letting the door slam shut behind us.

Something inside me eases. We're safe here, at least. No one can get to us. Perhaps a proper ruler of Demonheim could convince the realm to let them in, but we haven't had a proper ruler in so long that I'm not worried about that.

"Can I kiss you?" Heath blurts out.

"We're supposed to plan how to overthrow the king," I say slowly, but it's a weak protest even to my ears.

Heath takes a step closer, drawing into my space and holding my hand to his chest. "But consider this—we'll be much more focused and capable if we get this distraction out of the way."

I laugh, letting my fingers curl into the ties on his shirt. "I don't think it's possible to get the distraction out of the way. I somehow doubt one kiss could end the distraction." I doubt a thousand kisses could. It's like every nerve in my body is entirely attuned with his, even mere moments after meeting.

Heath grins wickedly at me, squeezing my hand, and his free hand comes up to latch onto my hip, pulling me even closer. "No one says it should be only one kiss."

I want to touch him. I want to grab that ridiculously soft looking hair; I want to mold myself to his broad chest. I want to feel those legs wrapped around my hips. I want everything from him, a desperate thrum under my skin that feels unnatural and yet so right.

"Kiss me, Chase," he whispers. "Please."

It's the soft please that convinces me, that causes me to lean closer without even truly thinking about it. I want this man. I want to taste him, to know him.

Mine. The thought echoes in my brain like a bell when our lips touch, and I reach up to hold his face to mine.

The skin-to-skin contact sets every nerve in my body alight. Mine. Mate.

Heath kisses me slowly, like he's hungry, like he's tasting me. Like I'm a meal for him to savor.

When at last we pull back, he grins at me, slow and dangerous. "I've waited six hundred years for that," he admits.

"Closer to eight, for me."

He blinks, then smiles. "Where have you been for the last six hundred years, then?"

"Here. Where else?" Where else would a demon be? We have two options. Demonheim, or a temporary pass to earth to trick other creatures—mostly hapless humans—into unfavorable bargains. That had been something I'd never had any particular inclination to do, so I'd been here.

He leans in to kiss me, and I have half a thought that he's making up for lost time. I can't say I blame him.

"Is that why demons seal deals with a kiss?" Heath asks, eyes intent on my mouth. "Are all demon kisses that drugging?"

He thinks my kiss is like a drug? Something inside me preens a bit, but then I remember the question and chuckle. "A demon can seal a deal with a handshake just as easily. Honestly, the magic doesn't require any such thing. It's the mating bond—we don't know our mates without the skin-to-skin contact. And no one is willing to accidentally ruin the life of their mate, or just miss knowing them entirely. So... the kiss. Just to be sure."

And after just one single kiss from this wolf, I understand why. It would gut me to know I never got this chance with him. He thinks my kiss is a drug? I think his is like grabbing onto lightning.

I haven't thought about my mate in years. There have been bigger things occupying my mind, and I hadn't wanted to think of anyone else in this mess with me. But now, it's like he's the only thing I can think about, taking over my vision of the future.

That forces me back to reality. "Hannah sent you?"

"Her and Ry—"

"Don't say his name," I interrupt, unintentionally but necessarily harsh. "They'll know. The realm responds to the king, the keeper of the keys. And he'll know."

"But Hannah's name is fine?"

My father is the type of man to disregard someone like Hannah. Not demon enough. Too female. He's wrong, and he'll realize it the hard way. It does make her name safe, though. "Her name is fine. Here. Not in front of others."

He raises an eyebrow. "I likely shouldn't be in front of others."

He has a point, considering he's so wolfish.

It's his size, mostly. I consider myself quite tall, but Heath is even bigger than me. With a well-built frame, shaggy dark hair, and watchful hazel eyes, I can practically see the wolf beneath his skin.

His presence feels different, too. While his energy is making my skin light up, I can imagine for other demons it'll be a beacon in the worst way. Demonheim isn't known for visitors, after all.

"We'll stay here until we have a plan," I agree.

Heath takes both my hands, walking himself backwards towards the sofa. "Sit with me."

Every inch of contact between us is distracting, but I nod anyway. I know that the future of Demonheim is dependent on our next actions, but somehow, I can't force myself to make a wiser choice.

Heath pulls me into his side, then buries his face in my neck, so I doubt I'm the only one distracted. "Sorry," he murmurs after a moment, but he's clearly not sorry enough, as his nose doesn't leave the crook of my neck. "Wolves like scent."

"What do I smell like?" I ask, automatically tilting my neck as if to give him better access.

"Like home," he says immediately, without any thought required. "Gods, Chase, if you knew—"

"I know your energy makes me feel more settled in my own skin than I ever have before," I say softly. "I think I understand."

He presses a kiss to my collarbone through my shirt. "Tell me more."

I almost do. I almost try to explain to a non-demon the feel of demon magic. I almost open my mouth and spill out the wild, insatiable urges burning through me right now.

"Not here," I force myself to say. "When this is done."

"When this is done," he agrees, but Heath keeps letting his nose drift along sensitive areas of my skin. I never knew the hinge of my jaw was so sensitive before Heath. And every time he touches me, the raw energy shooting through my body makes me feel like I could conquer the world.

"Tell me, what did Hannah—" I try to redirect our focus, but fail miserably the first time his hand ghosts over my thigh.

My head falls back and my eyes slip shut. I can feel my cock hardening in my trousers, desperate for Heath's touch.

We have a war to win. My father and his stupid sword and the unbelievable power it lends him must be stopped. We need to...

His hand slides higher on my thigh.

"We can't do anything until we know where the king will be," Heath murmurs. "Right?"

"Right," I agree absently, more focused on his fingers than anything else. Even through my trousers, his touch makes me shudder.

It would be more powerful if I were naked, though, and I'm seriously debating suggesting it when Heath interrupts my train of thought.

"Demon horns... they sensitive?"

"What?" I gasp, sure I somehow missed part of the conversation.

"Your horns, Chase. If I touch them, would you feel it?"

Gods, yes, I would. Short of fondling my cock, touching my horns is just about the most sexual thing he could do to me.

"Yes."

"Can I?"

"Touch them?" I ask, already slightly breathless.

"Yeah, Chase. Touch them. Lick them. Can I?"

I groan, closing my eyes, wondering if Heath knows exactly how fast I'm going to come all over him if he does that. "Please."

His fingers run through my hair, the touch delicate and soft and so at odds with what he's been saying that it would almost be relaxing if I could stop thinking about him licking my horns.

Then his fingers scrape over the base of them, and I curse, making Heath laugh huskily.

I don't know if it's his fingers or that laugh that makes me buck my hips, instantly and completely hard in my trousers.

When was the last time I was with someone? I can't even remember now, the thoughts driven completely out of my mind by the man next to me, stroking over my horns with a firm touch.

"Is this good?" Heath asks quietly.

"Gods, you..." I force myself to pull it together, to act like I'm centuries old and not born yesterday, green and desperate. "I believe you mentioned licking?"

Heath laughs again, low and husky and so desperately attractive. "Something you should know about wolves," he murmurs, his voice just as low and tempting as his laugh, "is that all of our senses are stronger. And we're always desperate to smell and taste our mates."

Before I can try to focus enough to ask any more, his lips press against my right horn, and his clever tongue runs along it, slow and sensual.

It's like lightning shooting through my body, and he knows exactly what he's doing.

I'm going to have to get him back later, to make him just as desperate, just as crazy and aching. But right now, I can only think of how his lips feel, teasing against the hard edge of my horn.

Heath hasn't touched my cock, yet I'm relatively positive I could come from this alone.

Thankfully, he doesn't make me find out, reaching his free hand down into my trousers while his lips and other hand continue to play with my horns. When he finally grabs my cock, I can't hold back any longer.

With just a single touch, I come all over him.

It takes me several long moments to come down from the high enough to remember to be embarrassed. Instead, I spend a long moment floating. The spark of his touch, the skill of his tongue, the completeness of him next to me—

When the feeling fades enough for embarrassment to creep in—I did just come with a single touch, after all, likely not leaving the best of first impressions—I turn to look at Heath. I plan to apologize, to promise that I'm not usually so quick off the mark, but the words are arrested in my throat, because he's licking his fingers clean.

And he's being careful to ensure he gets every damned drop.

His eyes catch mine, and he shrugs. "I told you. Wolves are always desperate for the taste of our mates."

Gods, that is... I don't have words. My brain completely fails me, abandoning me entirely to the image of Heath, of beautiful, rugged Heath, licking his fingers clean of my come.

Impossibly, I am relatively sure I could go again.

If this is what mating is, then I'm not sure how Heath and I are ever expected to be productive members of society again. I think hazily about a little house somewhere—somewhere outside of Demonheim—and just him and me, fucking, forever.

I think I could get used to a life like that.

I slide off my sofa and to my knees, reaching for his trousers.

He looks at me, a cross between amused and hungry. "Desperate to taste me, Chase? That seems a little wolf-ish."

"I can want to suck your cock without being a wolf." I wonder absently what it'll feel like. If his cock will give me the same thrill of pleasure any other contact between our skin does.

But before I can find out, a shock ripples through the air of Demonheim, stopping me in my tracks. It's the king, calling all of us to him.

Heath doesn't feel it, clearly, but he notices when I freeze. "Something happened."

I sigh, using his thighs to push myself upright. "That's our call to duty, sadly. I'll be returning to this later," I promise, looking down at his cock tenting his trousers. Then, half in promise and half out of curiosity, I slide my hand up his thigh, cupping his bulge for a moment before pulling my hand away. "But for now, we have a job to do."

Chapter Seven

Heath

I have never been so hard in my entire life. I have never wanted another being so much, so viscerally. My bones ache for him.

I want every inch of him to be on every inch of me. I want to hold him and smell him and touch him. I want to lick him, to taste every bit of him. One taste simply isn't enough, and I am desperate for more. My every thought is consumed by him, by his clever eyes and quick-moving hands, by those little horns that made him moan, and his druggingly sweet kisses.

My mate. The one person in the entire world that fate made perfectly for me, the person I'm meant for. And I have to sit here plotting how to dethrone a usurper king, like I can forget what he looked like on his knees, promises in his eyes, mere moments ago.

Life really isn't fair sometimes.

Still, overthrowing the king will get me closer to my goal of spending at least a month straight in bed with Chase, so I grit my teeth, will my cock to go down, and turn to work.

As plans go, it's not much of one. We've agreed that we have to strike now, one of the few times the sword will be out in the open, but other than that, our plan is relatively rudimentary.

"And it'll distract him enough that maybe I can get close and grab the sword. Then I can get it to you and you can slip away with it before he notices. I know it seems stupid to go after it in a crowd, but he's never without the sword, and we don't have a chance of sneaking up on him when he's alone. The crowd will be our only cover, especially with..." He trails off.

"Especially considering it'll be immediately obvious I'm not a demon," I conclude dryly. "Should we make me some fake horns? A costume, perhaps?"

I say it sarcastically, but his eyes trail over my body, a slow, careful perusal that I'd read as a sexual promise if his expression wasn't so serious. "I don't think you could ever trick someone into believing that you're a demon," he says.

"I thought not. Don't worry so much though—I'm very good at being where I shouldn't be. No one ever notices the difference." I've done it a thousand times. First by finding my way into matters of state, sneaking in behind my parents and managing to sit through entire council meetings without being noticed. Later, as an adult, by finding myself in more than one situation not dissimilar to this.

"The king isn't like other people," Chase says, his voice heavy.

"So this plan is doomed to fail? We should start again?" I demand. I'd be willing to start again, if Chase has a better idea. But if he doesn't, I'm not going to let risk to me be the reason we don't go forward.

He sighs. "No, no. We can do it," he vows.

He seems almost paralyzed with indecision, and I lean forward to grab his hand. "Listen to me. We're getting through this. Because we're finding a place after we've given over that damned sword, and you're going to fuck me senseless."

He stares at me, then licks his lips in a way that makes me groan. "With an offer on the table like that, how could I refuse?"

***

As confident as I sounded earlier, the truth is I have to fight off shaking as we enter the crowd.

So many demons. All of whom will easily be able to tell that I'm an outsider. Gods, even the damned realm knows I'm an outsider; the corridors and passageways are still nearly entirely unnavigable to me without Chase's guiding hand. All my skills for slipping into places unseen mean next to nothing here.

I hope my mate isn't set on staying together in Demonheim forever when this is all over, and not only because Celia will kill me if I don't come home. I've been in enemy war camps more hospitable than the halls of this place.

But still, this is what I was made for. I hold my breath and slip into the crowd behind Chase.

What I do isn't that remarkable. We're wolves, after all, and royal wolves at that. It shouldn't shock people we make use of some particularly wolfish traits.

Callum got the strength of the wolf, Celia the cunning. Bryce got the pack instincts, nipping at everyone's heels until they fall in line. And I got the predatory, graceful stealth, the muscles coiled right before a strike, right before the prey knows they're in danger.

This is no different, I remind myself. This is no different from any other time I've stalked my prey.

So I follow my mate into the fray, doing my best to look like I belong as the crowd closes in around us. Then, without a single word, Chase separates from me, sneaking closer to the king and leaving me to blend in with the crowd.

I hate being left to wait. I hate having no part in a plan, just needing to stand around and hope things work out.

Hope is not my strong suit.

"My people," The king begins, standing from his throne, set on a dais so he can overlook the room. The throne is as gaudy as the room, very clearly meant to resemble what the humans think of as hell. Did Demonheim come first, or is the king taking inspiration from other sources?

"We have struck a decisive blow against the agitators," he continues. He takes one step forward. It's one step further away from the sword, which rests against the throne. I stare, watching his legs, waiting to see if he'll keep moving.

"No longer can they invade our lands and steal away our loved ones," he continues. "The portal is now closed forever, guarded well."

Some cheers go up through the crowd. There's a distinct difference in the crowd, with one half rabidly hanging onto the false king's every word. The scene looks like so many I've seen late at night in grungy taverns, where drunken rabble cheers and bolsters the biggest bully they can find. Their words seem to push him higher, and in turn his continuing rhetoric makes them practically froth at the mouth in their enthusiasm. It's a never-ending, self-perpetuating cycle.

Never mind that they're wrong. They might think they closed off the portal, but my presence here says that's very much not true. All that tells me is that Ryder is more powerful than his father.

Of course, this type of crowd isn't here to discuss that type of nuance.

But in their near-rabid ferocity, they miss the others among them. The ones with shifty eyes, who stand still, trying nearly as hard as I am to not be noticed.

Maybe they didn't manage to join Ryder's rebels before the portal was supposedly closed to them. But I think if they had half a chance, they'd be gone.

"But our realm needs more," the king continues, oblivious to those who are a moment from snapping. Or perhaps not oblivious. Perhaps he just thinks the demons on his side outweigh anything they might be able to do. "Our realm is strong, yes, but it is a demanding realm. It needs power. It needs you all."

I've been purposefully avoiding looking at Chase, not wanting to draw attention to him, but I can't resist him a moment longer. I've been able to feel where he is the entire time even without looking, a combination of his delicious scent and a new, intuitive sense for his very presence.

Is this what being a mate means? Carving out a permanent space for him in my mind, always knowing exactly where he is, always desperate to have him back at my side when he isn't there?

He's gotten close, moving behind the throne. I bite my lip, calculating angles. Where is the best intercept point in this gaudy throne room? I need it to be convenient for Chase, while also close to the exit. I also need to avoid moving too much before it's time to truly flee, lest someone figure out what I am.

I do my best to be like smoke, intangible and unnoticeable, slipping a little further back into the crowd, trying to predict the angle he will leave at, hoping he's as aware of me as I am of him.

The roar in the room reaches a fever pitch, and I know, even without ever having worked with him before, that this is the moment Chase will choose to strike. I watch him creep closer behind his father, watch him reach out for the sword, and then watch his father's hand move in a way that startles Chase back. I wince, then hope it isn't an obvious enough movement to draw anyone's attention.

I've been at war too many times in my life not to know battles like this are won and lost on seconds. We need seconds of distraction, seconds to get the sword away before someone else realizes exactly what just happened. We only need seconds to either slaughter the king or run with the sword.

We only need seconds to lose our opportunity.

Chase screws up his face, and I know without even speaking to him that he's fully aware that might have been our only chance. Still, Chase reaches forward again, as if determined to make this opportunity work for us.

No, I want to shout, though thankfully I keep my mouth shut. We can go back. We can regroup. We can try again another day.

But Chase doesn't hear my thoughts. He reaches forward, and just as I see his hand getting close, his father gesticulates grandly, half-turning to face the other part of his audience.

Half-turning directly towards Chase.

I know what I have to do before I even consciously think to do it. It's instinctive the same way following his scent was. This is my mate, and I can't let anything happen to him.

And I'll pay any price for him.

I move just enough to make the people around me aware of my presence, alerting them that something is not quite right in their midst.

I think for half a second that Celia is going to kill me for getting myself in this much trouble. Then I think of her complete adoration of Bethany, and think maybe she would understand.

Maybe she'll even forgive me eventually, if I die here today.

I step forward, parting the crowd with my large frame, moving closer to the front.

It starts with whispers. Then, as the whispers spread through the crowd, more and more people turn to look at me.

I hope Chase can tell what's going on. I hope he knows it's time to pull back. That I've taken their attention for the moment, but he needs to use it to save himself.

The king turns to look at me. "And who is this?" His voice seems to practically shake the surrounding room. I force myself to look him directly in the eyes.

Let him focus on me. Let him lash out at me. Anything, as long as he doesn't turn around.

I don't answer him. I just stare at him, waiting to see what his next move will be.

All the angles I calculated towards the exit just minutes before are now useless. Running through the crowd won't save me. Not that my wolf would let me leave the sweet, luring scent of my mate behind.

I purposefully don't look at him, don't draw any attention to him. But it's hard, and all the wolf inside me wants to do is check that he's okay.

But right now, I'm the biggest danger to him.

The king looks at me and laughs. The sound carries so much menace that I force myself to lock all my muscles so I don't react. I can't let him see me flinch.

I won't let him see me flinch. I am a prince, a warrior. I won't cower before him.

"This is the best my son can do?" he asks incredulously, taking his eyes off me to look around the room as if he and his rabid followers are in on the same joke. "He can't even get a demon to work for him. Do you see the failure that my son is? Demonheim has rejected him, and he has gone begging to the wolves, disgracing himself."

I wish I had prepared something to say, anything, but I'm not the speech-maker. For that we'd need Celia or Bryce, but instead there's only me, and I just keep staring the king down, aching to look over at Chase, to see if he slipped away, if he managed to re-join the crowd fully, doing whatever it takes to cast suspicion off of himself.

But I don't look. I just stare straight ahead.

"What shall we do with the lost little puppy?" The king says when it becomes clear I won't speak. He reaches back for the sword, and I force myself not to look away. "Death seems too quick. Let us send a message to my son."

Chase appears at the foot of the dais, as if he just arrived there. "The cages," he says, and I think I can detect a quaver in his voice, but I hope no one else can. "If your majesty agrees."

He's silent for a moment, contemplating, but at last he nods. "A fine idea. The cages it is. Chase, if you will—"

I don't react, but inside I relax. He believes Chase. He thinks Chase is on his side.

Chase comes up to me. "Will you go quietly, or will it be death after all?" he says for our audience, but I hear the message.

Trust me.

And I do. I, who have only ever trusted my siblings, trust Chase with my whole heart, my mind, my very life. Never mind that we only met hours ago. I know what he tastes like, will never get his sweet smell out of my nostrils, know his face when he comes, know the intensity of his eyes when he plans. I want everything with him, and I trust him now.

I cross my own arms behind my back, indicating he can lead me out, securing my wrists in place. He grabs me, his touch gentler than is probably wise, given our current audience.

Then he pushes me ahead of him.

I don't turn my head, but I hear footsteps behind us. Guards, likely. A wise choice, because in any other circumstance, I'd certainly kill my captor and be gone already.

But I just let Chase lead me, hoping his grip on my wrists isn't my last chance to feel his touch.

He's walking very close behind me as a consequence of pinning my wrists like he is, and it gives us the perfect opportunity to talk after we exit the throne room. "The cages are awful," he murmurs lowly. "But no one can hurt you. No one can reach you. The king can't hurt you." I can feel the quick squeeze of his hand, and I force myself not to react.

"I'll come back for you as soon as I can," he promises. "Just hold on, okay? Remember I'm coming back. It'll help."

Then we come to a stop in front of a large door, made of heavy, tarnished metal and reeking like death.

My heart rate picks up, and I know Chase can feel it. He squeezes my wrists again.

A guard moves forward to unlock it, then Chase shoves me inside as gently as he can without looking suspicious.

I turn around, getting one last look at Chase before the door is slammed shut in my face.

Then, there is nothing.

Chapter Eight

Chase

I force myself to keep breathing as I walk away from the cages. I force myself to keep my features even, like this means nothing to me, like I'm not screaming on the inside.

My mate. I had done that to my mate. The thought shakes through me, rattling my bones with its wrongness. I had condemned him to a fate that many consider worse than death, an endless, prolonged torment, a complete isolation from the outside world, from your own body and mind. It's enough to drive a man mad.

And if I don't get him out, and soon, that is the fate awaiting my mate.

And it's all my fault.

I see it flashing before my eyes. Sneaking up behind my father, my grab for the sword, the scare and me pulling back, my foolish decision to try again. And then Heath making the decision to sacrifice himself for me.

My mate. The courageous, selfless love he had shown—

I realize abruptly I've stopped walking, then a hand clasps me on the back. Fariq's nails dig into my shoulder, and I hold still to resist bucking him off.

"Making quite a name for yourself," he notes quietly, so the guards who escorted Heath and I to the cages can't overhear. "Two acts of bravery in as many days. Anyone would think you're a bonafide hero, Chase."

The petty jealousy of who gets more of our pathetic father's attention is mind-boggling to me, but I know it's life and death in Fariq's mind. I suppose bastard born sons who have no hope of benefitting the family line have to have something, after all.

"I do what I can for our king," I murmur. It's a good thing words praising the king have become so deeply ingrained in me, because I doubt I could come up with a novel thought right now.

Not when my entire brain is consumed with thoughts of Heath. Heath, who has been in the cages mere minutes but is already suffering for it. How long will it take the harm to be irreversible? How long until he forgets me, forgets everything?

No. He did it for me. An act of devotion so mind-bogglingly deep, I doubt I would have understood it in the slightest before the mating bond formed between us. And I will find a way to return that level of love. I have to.

I shrug Fariq's hand off my shoulder, mutter excuses, and retreat to my room.

I manage to close the door, sealing out the world, before I fall to my knees and begin to hyperventilate.

***

I don't know how much time has passed before I can gather myself. All I know is that every minute is another minute I leave my mate to suffer in the cages.

Gods, the cages.

It was the best option, I know. My father and his loyal followers like Fariq can be ruthless, and I don't want to think of what torture they might have dreamed up for the werewolf who just fell into their laps. At least Heath isn't being hurt.

He's just being driven mad.

Heath is strong, I try to remind myself. He'll keep himself together as long as possible.

But that doesn't mean anything and I know it. Nearly everyone thrown in the cages is strong. Presumably, they all break in there. That's what the cages are meant for.

And Heath is a wolf. I've never seen a wolf in the cages before—they tend to take care of their own, not needing demon intervention—but I imagine the complete isolation of the cage will be hard on a pack creature.

If I've ruined him, if I broke this before we even started—

I shudder, then refuse to let myself think about it.

***

My father summons me again, the thrum of the call rattling my bones.

I can't ignore it. I can't have him ask any questions, even as I desperately wish to avoid him.

So I pull myself together, casting a quick glamor to make myself look as fine as I can. The energy demand of even this small magic rocks me, but it can't be helped. The magic isn't strong, but no one ever looks closely enough to see through it.

Here I am, Chase, bastard son, enthusiastic participant in the day-to-day life of Demonheim, supporter of the king. Totally fine, and not ruffled in the slightest from the altercation earlier.

Because nothing bothers me, as far as my father is concerned. And it's in my best interest to keep it that way.

"You called for me, my king?" I ask, stepping into the throne room once more.

I try my absolute hardest to not let my eyes linger on that damned sword. Instead, I focus on the room. On my father on this throne, on several of his advisors standing around the dais, and the dark, palpable energy buzzing through the room.

Whatever this is, I already don't like it.

"Did the wolf say anything before you locked him away?" he asks, nodding to me as I step into the place left for me.

"He said I would regret it," I say slowly, weighing my options. Heath was silent in the face of my father, but any of those guards might have seen him and I speaking before I put him in the cages. "But nothing more specific."

The king heaves a deep sigh. "My son is becoming more of a nuisance," he says, and despite him having a host of sons in this room, we all know who he means without having to ask. "And it's high time I did something about it, don't you think?"

Something like get out of his way? I don't say it, however much I want to.

I barely know my brother. I was never meant to associate with the likes of him. But even without knowing Ryder, even while I couldn't claim him as a friend or even really a brother, I know he will be a better ruler than our father.

"What would you have us do, your majesty?" Fariq asks, voice half breathless like he really hangs on the king's every word.

The king's attention turns from me to Fariq. "You were in charge of creating a plan of attack." The words are crisp and demanding. He's not angry yet, but we can all hear it brewing underneath.

His eyes widen. "I—we're factoring how to work the portal into our plan."

"Can you open it?"

"I'm confident we'll discover how."

There's nothing to discover, I'm relatively confident. It only ever opened for me because Demonheim likes me. I don't say anything, of course.

I'm barely listening. I'm too busy watching the keys on the king's belt, eyes stuck to the one I know unlocks the cages.

It's hopeless. I know it's hopeless. Even so, I can't help but watch, letting the sinking pit of despair inside me open deeper and deeper with each passing second.

CHAPTER NINE

HEATH

There is nothing.

It is not darkness. It is not quiet. This is not the absence of something.

It is the total, complete lack of it in the first place.

Time ceases to exist as soon as that gate slams shut. Or maybe not: maybe it is hours later before I lose any sense of it. I'll never be able to tell.

I forget what colors look like. I know they exist; I remember the idea of them—the golden brown of my siblings' eyes, the sandy shade of Chase's hair, the crisp white snow on the mountains around my home—but I simply can't make my brain remember what they actually look like. The words rattle around in my head, taking all my energy, trying to make the concepts turn into anything of value and failing.

I try to hold on to that crisp apple scent of my mate. I can frame it in my mind, or at least a facsimile of it. But I've known since the moment the door clanged shut that it's just a memory. It's not real.

I've always been the loner Crae sibling, the one who can go off for weeks or months without any problem. I've felt comfortable in my solitude.

I've been a fool. I haven't known what solitude is.

For the first time in my life, I am truly, completely, entirely alone.

I've forgotten why I'm here.

There was a me before all this, I'm certain. A me who existed, who had plans and goals and things to live for. All of that seems so far away, so distant now. It's not worth holding onto.

Here, in this cage, nothing is worth holding onto. I am nothing. I have nothing. Nothing exists outside of this very narrow here and now, not really.

There is no world. I just exist, for a certain value of existing.

There is darkness, complete, utter darkness. Not the darkness of the night I think I can remember. This is just the darkness of nothing.

Except those eyes. Sometimes, when I look up, there are eyes peering from the darkness into my soul. But then they vanish, and there is nothing once more.

Perhaps this is all there is. Perhaps I'm wrong, when I get those hazy impressions of more, of a before, of people—of two tall men, dark hair and golden eyes and the same smile, of a woman almost as tall, her eyes too serious, of a woman with her, tall and stick-thin and blonde, of a man, with little black horns and so much goodness coiled up in him—perhaps those are all just dreams.

Dreams? What are dreams? What does that mean?

And then my wolf takes control.

***

Our wolves only force their way forward when we're in severe, nearly unsalvageable distress. The animal part of us is always so much more adept at survival than we could ever be, after all.

But it is an animal. More than that, it's a wild part of ourselves, completely uncontrollable, looking out for nothing but the best interest of the wolf and the pack. Or at least, so I've heard. The wolf taking over is extremely rare, and I've only ever heard second hand about it.

I suppose I shouldn't be shocked. If there was ever a wolf in emotional distress, it would be me.

But my thoughts are clearer now. Perhaps the animal brain is simpler, able to cut through all the nonsense. Perhaps it's that the wolf's senses are even stronger than mine. Perhaps it's just that the magic isn't meant to contain the transformed wolf. Either way, I feel more myself as an animal than I did as a man.

I can put names to the faces I saw. I can remember my past.

I can remember how I got here, and what I still need to do.

The wolf stands—and I hadn't even realized I was lying on the ground—and shakes its coat, ready for action.

The wolf is looking for something, I realize.

Those eyes might not have been a hallucination.

***

The wolf in me hates this place.

The cages aren't strong enough to deaden the senses of the wolf fully, but it's still oppressive. A wolf's senses should take in a thousand times more than a human, and the wolf whines, knowing something is being kept from it.

But it's not gone. Just muted. And that's more than my human form had.

My fur stands on end, the wolf whining again, side-stepping, trying frantically to take in this new world.

Eyes, again. And then they're gone, leaving me to doubt if they ever even existed in the first place.

The darkness is nearly impenetrable, even for the wolf. The cage is loaded with too many scents for the wolf to parse through, and there is still absolutely no sound.

I am a predator. I am supposed to be the most lethal predator, the perfect combination of human dexterity with a wolf's strength, power, and honed instincts, trained to perfection and able to take on any challenge.

And I'm stopped by some darkness.

Whining, the wolf curls into a ball and refuses to move.

***

The footsteps break the deafening silence like thunder claps. The only sound I've heard since this started besides my own whine—and even that had sounded oddly muted—the echoing footsteps shake me from my stupor.

Still, the wolf doesn't want to move. Get up and fight, you stupid beast, I think, but even my snarl is half-hearted at best. What's the point in this place, after all?

The footsteps stop, and at last I'm able to focus on a singular scent, honing in on the figure in front of me.

She crouches down, and, with a clear lack of self-preservation, puts her hand on my head.

"Come, little wolf," she croons, her words soft but her voice jagged from disuse. "Come see."

CHAPTER TEN

HEATH

The wolf snaps at her. Any reasonable person would back away quickly.

This clearly is not a reasonable person, because she coos at the wolf and continues to pet me like a dog.

"Manners," she scolds when I snap again.

The wolf cocks our head, studying her. This close the wolf can see a small amount, making out the dark form of a woman seemingly too small to live. Even so, her eyes glow an eerie blue, like lightning splitting the sky. Her scent, clean linen buried under dirt and decay, chokes the air around both of us.

Somewhere, the wolf crosses into curiosity about this stranger, and I remember where I am.

How long has she been here?

"You'll feel better if you know where you are," she says, voice sickeningly soothing once more. "I hear wolves like that, yes? Checking perimeters, knowing your territory."

She's not wrong, per se. And as much as I hate to admit it, those wolfish instincts are firmly in charge at the moment. The wolf fights the desperation-induced lethargy to stand and follow her.

She's like a beacon, the only thing on the entire horizon that I can perceive. Even with her presence I can't make out more than passing details in the world around us. But her scent remains a constant, something soothing under all the rot and decay. And when she deigns to face me, her eyes are something I couldn't possibly miss.

So I follow her in a circle, having to check my pace repeatedly so I don't simply walk right past her and leave her behind, and hope she'll begin to give me a clue about what exactly is going on.

She doesn't talk for an indeterminate amount of time. I have no hope of actually knowing how long, not here, where minutes and years feel interchangeable. Then her voice breaks the silence like a whip crack, sharp and startling. "The first thing to know about the cages is that the title is a lie."

The wolf watches her, unable to ask for clarification, just following along behind her and hoping she'll explain. Hoping this is not just the ramblings of a madwoman.

Then again, would it be fair for me to expect anything else? If she's been here longer than I have, and I've already lost control over my body to the wolf—

No, I wouldn't be able to blame her if she only spoke in half-formed thoughts and nonsense.

"It's only one cage," she clarifies, like she suddenly remembers she had been speaking. "All different entrances, all different cells. All connected, like veins in the body. Most never know, too trapped in their mind. But we know. You and I know."

Maybe she's mad. But this place certainly feels bigger than any cell I've ever seen.

Then again, she could have me walking in tiny little circles, like an animal on a lead rope, and I'd have no way to tell the difference.

"We know," she says again, nodding like she said something wise. "Hm, little wolf? All you needed was a reminder that there is still a living creature in you, hm? A smart one too, I bet."

Not knowing how to respond to that—and being unable to even if I knew what to say—I just continue to follow the lightning-eyed creature, wondering what she'll deign to tell me next.

***

"Little wolf, can you smell this place?" she eventually asks me.

Little wolf is beginning to grate on me. I stand well past her hip, and this woman should not be accusing others of being little, not when she's a twig of a thing.

Wasted, emaciated, and withered. Not to mention the rotting, pervasive scent of death and decay clinging to her skin.

I don't answer her. I can't, after all.

She sighs. "I was hoping you could scent the others."

Others?

She doesn't explain for a while. Then, "These cages are so full, so disgustingly full. But they rot away, and I can't find them when they're that far gone. So it's just you and I, unless you can find them when I can't."

Rot away?

She seems to know what I'm thinking about. Or perhaps her lost mind just happens to be meandering down the same path as mine.

"We won't rot, you and I," she assures me. "Even after everything, Demonheim still loves me. And you... well, the wolf will protect you, won't it?"

It's not reassuring that it comes out like a question. The wolf is protecting me so far. But will it continue to do so?

Trapped animals give up and die. I've seen it before, a thousand times, hunting for dinner and delivering a mercy kill before the animal's misery can tear it apart.

The wolf might be protecting me now, but I know it can't last forever. The restlessness building beneath my skin, the denial of my very senses—I can already feel the wolf losing control.

I try to force the wolf into making a concerted effort to find any potential others, but all the wolf can find is the rot that pervades this place. If those lost souls she mentioned truly did just rot away, their scent would blend in with hers easily enough.

Is that what this place does? Cause you to give up, curl up on your side, and literally wait to rot away? I shudder just thinking about it, then force the wolf to match this woman's pace even more closely.

I will not be separated from her.

"Demonheim, Demonheim, Demonheim," she says, her voice a mournful sing-song. "Why have you left me here?"

Her evident grief makes the wolf want to bay. I wish I could see her as more than just a vague outline of shapes and her eyes, so I could confirm my building suspicion. Are there horns on her head?

I've never heard of demons locking their own in the cages. The cages are for the truly, unchangeably wicked among us, an eternal punishment for a creature that either can't be killed, or who deserves eternal suffering more than a merciful death.

And demons, I've heard, cull their own. They don't let their own get so bad that they need the cages. They, more than anyone, are aware of how bad the cages can be.

There should not be a demon here. There should not be a woman mournfully mumbling about how much she loves Demonheim, and how much the realm loves her.

Then again, perhaps she's just mad. How can she claim Demonheim loves her when this is where she is? She's as trapped as I am, after all.

"My beloved home," she mutters again. "Would you do this to me?"

Her despair seems to grow as she keeps muttering, until I hear her physically striking herself and know I need to intervene. Mad or not, this woman is the only company I have.

I nudge my head into her side, trying to draw her attention.

It works, rather unfortunately, because she strokes me behind the ears like I'm some sort of spoiled dog, and I have to fight to keep the wolf from snapping her fingers off.

"I know, I know," she says softly, soothingly, as if I'm the one who needs comfort, as if she has forgotten her own worry already.

"The world is a cruel place, but we need to have hope," she nods. "Yes, yes."

Hope? What exactly are we hoping for?

Chase. The name comes unbidden to my mind, stronger than anything else down here.

I shove it down. I need to hope he lives, that he has the good sense to stay away from here. If the king catches him near the cages, would he throw him in here along with me, just to prove a point?

"I thought he'd come for me," my companion says mournfully, and I realize we've stopped walking. There's no difference down here, no change in scenery. The only true difference is the motion of my legs, and even that is oddly muted, although whether that's the cages or the wolf controlling my body is hard to say. "I thought it couldn't be forever."

She thought *who* would come for her?

Anyone, I suppose. Anyone trapped here would hope a loved one would care enough to save them. Even I can't quash the traitorous thoughts of Chase or Celia suddenly appearing before me.

"He's not my mate," she confides in me, as if I have any idea who she is speaking about. "My mate would have come for me. All I would have had to do was call his name, and... poof!" she says, followed by the sound of her fingers snapping.

I hear movement, then see her crouch to the ground, sitting in front of me. "The others at least talked, for a time," she sighs. "It was much more invigorating."

Say something, you dumb animal, I curse at the wolf.

I manage a hesitant little yip, which really isn't worth anything, but then the woman pets me again, and I decide to allow it.

If she gives up on me, if she leaves me behind—

The very thought makes me ache. I remember what I was, left here alone in this miserable, oppressive nothingness. This woman with the lightning eyes lights the way like nothing else will, and if letting her pet me a bit is the cost of keeping her close, then it's a small price to pay.

But only behind the ears. I'm not rolling over for belly rubs like some mutt.

Still, even her petting is listless, almost thoughtless, and she doesn't rise again.

The smell of rot only gets worse.

CHAPTER ELEVEN

HEATH

I can't convince her to rise again.

Instead, she lays down on her back, hand loose in my fur, and just talks.

"He wasn't my mate," she confesses again, and I'm not even sure if she knows she's said it before. "And once you find your mate you should know better, know that no one else will ever compare, but I was sad, and lonely. But my mate would have come for me. I would have called his name and he would have been here. And that's the difference, isn't it?"

I think briefly of my sister, who would walk through fire and fight a thousand battles to reach Bethany's side. I think of what I'd been willing to do for Chase, even after knowing him for such a short time.

She continues, petting the wolf's fur in the wrong direction, and I have to leash the beast from snapping at her. "I would have come for him too, of course. In a heartbeat. I've always thought it so wonderful, that the magic just lets us be there for our mates. No cost, no penalty. No rules. Like nothing, not even the strictest rules that make up our magic, can stop mates from being together. Isn't it beautiful?"

Wolves believe our mates are fate-chosen, perfect for us. That nothing and no one can get between you and your mate. Not even the pack, the second most sacred order in our worlds. And now I hear that demon magic bows to the very same principles, more or less. It's somewhat reassuring.

She sighs. "Just call his name and poof! He'd come."

Her voice is feeble by the end, trailing off, getting lost in this place. The wolf growls at her, but it's not a threat. It's a reminder to stay with us.

But she doesn't respond, leaving me to think about her story.

Does she mean call his name literally?

It's not something I can even test, because the wolf can only communicate in grunts and growls, and none of those are even remotely close to Chase's name. I can think of his name as hard as I want, screaming it in my mind, but I can now say for certain that doing so isn't enough to bring him to my side.

So I need to convince the wolf to let me go, a task easier said than done.

I've only ever heard about a wolf fully transforming, but all the stories say the wolf needs reassurances, that it won't let the werewolf go until it is sure they are once more safe. And I could never be considered safe right now.

I'm more capable than you at getting us out of this, I try to convince the wolf. It doesn't budge.

I try cajoling, wheedling, and thinking the situation over to myself repeatedly, trying to convince the animal part of my mind to see my point of view. I try forcing the change, trying to wrest back control, and get nowhere.

The wolf is stronger than me. That's an uncomfortable realization; I've rarely not been the strongest one in any situation. There is something inside of me that is stronger than me, that can control me and take over my body, and I can't fight it away.

That's not a fair thought; the wolf doesn't intend to hurt me, after all. The wolf is a manifestation of myself, my own form of magic in a way, and it's meant only to protect me. The wolf doesn't know anything else. It will do anything to protect me and mine, my mate and my pack. That's all it can do. That's all it will ever do.

I still don't like that I've ceded control of my body to it. Especially now, when I so desperately need that control.

As I continue to argue with a wolf that can't communicate in words, my companion just lies there. I know she's there and still alive because her eyes remain open, glowing as she stares into nothing. I don't know if it's her presence, the beacon that it is, or my own newfound determination that keeps me going, but at least I can say the worst effects of the cages are kept at bay.

The same, unfortunately, cannot be said for her. She lays there listlessly, only breaking her silence to mourn her mate not coming for her in short, sad bursts that inevitably fade away to nothing.

But it's when she starts chanting a name that I double my resolve.

This will get us to your mate, I try to tell the wolf.

And for just a second, I feel the wolf's control waver. But then it's back, matched by a resolve not in words but that I understand, nonetheless.

I am better equipped to help our mate than you are, I reassure the wolf. Trust me to save us. Trust him.

It whines, long and low and truly pitiful, but I can already feel it happening. I can feel the wolf letting me go.

I come gasping into my human form, desperate for air like I just completed a feat of strength, even if I haven't moved. "Chase," I rasp out, my voice broken from long disuse. "Chase," I plead, layering every intention, every desperate longing, into my words. "Chase."

CHAPTER TWELVE

CHASE

The call feels like a lover's caress.

When my father calls, it is firm, unyielding, pressing on me in a way I could never ignore, as much as I may want to.

But this is different. This call is as persistent as my father's, yes, but it's gentle in a way I've never felt before. Coaxing, perhaps, like a soft croon calling me away.

I don't think; I just give in. I close my eyes, and it's like the magic is at my fingertips already, like I don't even need to find it. And then I'm gone.

When I re-materialize, I know where I am before I open my eyes. I've never been in the cages before, but every demon knows about them. They feel wrong, like Demonheim has abandoned us here. The energy and magic that crackles around the realm, feeding our life force just as we feed it, simply isn't here.

When I open my eyes, all I see is a strange blue glow, which all but confirms my suspicions.

I fight down the panic building inside me. I'm in the cages, but it's not permanent. I can get out. I will get out. I must be able to.

I'm here for a reason. That call did not steer me wrong.

"Heath?"

"Chase?" The sound comes from at my feet. "Oh, thank the gods, that worked, I didn't—" A ragged breath that might be a repressed sob cuts through the thick, oppressive air. "She was babbling about being able to call her mate here, but how it didn't work, and I thought—well, it worked, clearly."

"It worked," I repeat dumbly. "Who told you?"

"Her," he says, and I get the sense that he's pointing, but of course I see nothing. He huffs. "I could see an outline when I was still in wolf form. Now it's just her eyes, and she stopped talking a while ago."

"You were in your wolf form?" I demand.

"The wolf deemed this place dangerous to my health and safety," Heath says, and I think he's attempting to be sarcastic, although his words fall flat. "And it still does. And now the wolf definitely is upset that you're here, because now you're in danger too. I'm fighting it, and I'm not winning. Chase, if we can—"

His speed picks up as he keeps talking, like he's in a rush to get the words out. I want to touch him, reassure him, but I can't even find him in the absolutely blinding dark of the cages. And, more to the point, I don't have reassuring news to share.

"I don't know if I can get us out," I admit. "The magic that got me in—whoever is with you was right, demons can consider calling their name to be a primitive contract, enough for a summoning of sorts, and the mating bond is already essentially a tool to help magnify my power, so it makes sense that you can call a mate into the cages even though no one is supposed to be able to get in and out except through the door. But out is harder. Because you can't call me out, by nature of us being, well, in."

I hope Heath understands that. I've been told that demon magic is confusing and nearly unintelligible to non-demons, although personally I think our strict adherence to rules makes it more intelligible than any other form of magic. But Heath is silent for a moment before saying, "You understand that none of that is helping me hold the wolf at bay."

I know, I want to say, but I also don't have a better answer for him, because lying to a man who can turn into a deadly beast and is a hairsbreadth from doing so seems like a poor plan.

But before I can think up some sort of answer, I hear a pained whine, then a little yip as a furred head rubs against my side.

Oh, gods. He's a wolf again. I'm now trapped in the cages with a wolf.

"Easy there," I murmur. There's a wolf in here, and the wolf might share a body with my mate, but I'd be a fool to think that makes me safe.

Wolves aren't supposed to actually be wolves. And if they are, everything I know tells me to run like hell.

But I'm trapped here, and, as far as I can tell, there is nowhere to go. I hold very, very still. Maybe he'll ignore me.

The soft fur on his back nudges at my arm, and then I feel a pressure on my legs.

I take a deep breath. He's walking around me, pressing his body against mine in a tight little circle.

Is he herding me? Is he scenting me?

Either way, the wolf doesn't seem inclined to hurt me, so something in me relaxes slightly. "If you'd given me a moment, I would have told you that I can still try," I tell where I think the wolf is. "You're a little reactive, huh?"

A cold nose nudges my hand. "Sure, sure," I agree, half hysterical now. A giant wolf is nudging me gently. Is he playing with me? Is he attempting to soothe me? As soon as the thought crosses my mind, I know it's true. The giant beast that took over my mate's body is not going to hurt me. Just the opposite, in fact.

"So, I need you to hold still," I tell him, and then am surprised when the wolf actually listens. He freezes like ice has encased him, like any single twitch will be the end of us. "Alright, and then…" I put my hand on what I think is his neck. Then I see the mysterious glowing eyes, the only spot of color and light down here, and impulsively reach for whoever it is.

It might be a mistake, considering that creatures don't tend to get locked into the cages for no good reason. But if she really did help Heath—

I can't leave someone who helped my mate behind. I reach for her too, getting a hand on her, and then close my eyes. It doesn't make much of a difference regarding sight down here in the cages, but it does help me visualize where I want to go and visualize the magic taking us there.

And then it feels like getting ripped apart.

Chapter Thirteen

Heath

I barely have time to be angry at being a wolf again—and embarrassed that my mate saw me lose control like that—before Heath is doing something.

I don't know what exactly he plans, but his hands land on me, and then I feel a ripple pass through me.

And then we're gone.

***

We land in what I recognize as Chase's room, the three of us sprawled on the floor. Suddenly having my senses fully returned to me is overwhelming, and I have to close my eyes, whining as sounds and scents assault me.

The world hums. There's a sound to it, an ebb and flow, a gentle background noise that is simply unnoticeable, unless you've been forced to adapt to its absence.

And the smell... something besides the rot of the cages is more than welcome, even as it's overwhelming.

I take deep, even breaths, using the scent of my mate to center me. Out. I'm out, I'm free, I'm with Chase, and anything is possible from here.

It's then that I realize Chase being silent is probably not a good thing.

I force my eyes open, turning my head to look at where his scent is strongest, only to find him unconscious.

Fuck.

A wolf is not the best caretaker for an unconscious immortal with no obvious injury. I can at least smell for blood, I suppose—of which there is none—but I don't have any hands to move him to somewhere more comfortable than the damned floor.

I look over at the woman, my guide and companion in the cages. She's unconscious too, although that might have been true before Chase did whatever he did.

I look her over, checking for blood and injuries. She's small, painfully thin, with dark hair that does nothing to hide the dark horns poking out of her head.

So I was right. She's a demon. What the hell was a demon doing trapped in the cages?

She smells like rot still. It doesn't smell fresh, but rather like the scent simply clings to her. Other than that, I can't detect anything wrong with her.

I need to get Chase into bed, and just hope that all he needs is rest. But I can't, because I don't have hands.

Fucking wolf. I curse out the beast inside me, but it doesn't react. It doesn't seem to care. I'm sure it thinks it's doing the right thing, that it's protecting us.

I huff and circle the two unconscious forms once more. Nothing is changing, so I instead force the wolf to lie down in front of the door, guarding them from the world outside.

And then I close my eyes and pass out.

***

When I wake, glowing blue eyes are inches away from my face.

My human face, I realize. The wolf has let me go. "Hello," I say, voice thick with sleep. My head aches bitterly, and I wonder if it's a side effect of the cages or turning from human to wolf to human to wolf to human.

"Home," she says, such ecstasy on her face that it's almost uncomfortable to look at.

"Home," I agree with her, although this place certainly doesn't feel like home to me. The best that can be said for it is it smells like my mate.

My mate. Chase. I force myself to sit upright, the motion sending my head spinning, and peer around my companion for my mate.

He's there. He's still unconscious, right on the ground, and the sight looks far too close to a corpse for my liking. "Is he okay?" I demand, although I doubt this woman has any more information than I do.

"His energy is drained," she murmurs, casting a vague look at him. "What you asked him for was too much, wolf."

"How do I help him?"

"Give him time. That's all you can do." She tilts her head. "And hold him. He'll like that."

Time. I hate the idea, because I can't forget for a minute where we are. We're in Demonheim, and Chase's room might feel relatively safe, but this is the heart of enemy territory, technically. Chase's damned father could be right outside that door.

We don't have time. We need to regroup and plan how to reorganize our efforts. We have a job to do.

But I can't magically make him better, unfortunately, so I look over at my unconscious mate once more. "Can I help him any other way?"

"You are," she says, and her eyes dart around the room so fast that I'm shocked she's at all able to keep track of our conversation. "Mates provide energy for their mates. If he didn't have you, he wouldn't have survived what he attempted. Let him rest. Don't leave." She gives me a crooked, ugly smile. "Mates are important, wolf. Like mine." She looks lost. "Where is my mate?"

She's gone again, and I can't blame her after however long in the cage, but I also don't know how to help her. "Don't leave," I order her, and force myself to my feet.

I sway there for a moment, trying to make the world realign itself. When I can see straight, I make my way across the room, finding Chase and lifting him.

I can't help but bury my face in his hair, inhaling that crisp apple scent. I shudder, inhaling again. It smells like home, like hope and promise.

I carry him through the door I haven't gone through yet, hoping it leads to a bedroom. Relieved to find that it does, I lay him carefully on the bed, removing his boots.

I leave the rest of his clothes in place, even as I'm tempted to keep making him more comfortable. I don't want him to wake up from unconsciousness to find himself undressed when he won't remember getting that way.

No, the first time I get Chase truly naked, we'll both certainly remember the day.

Then, though I hate to do it, I kiss his forehead and leave the room.

It feels like an absence again, even though I could be back at his side in less than ten steps. I grit my teeth against the ache and force myself to move.

I move the sofa in front of the door. I don't know if it'll stop anyone from getting in who truly wishes to, but that's not my primary motive for doing so.

I want to stop the woman still calling for her mate from wandering out.

"Stay here," I remind her again. "Get some rest. We can help you when Chase is awake."

And then I return to my mate, slipping into bed beside him, and finally feeling settled again once I'm holding him in my arms.

Chapter Fourteen

Chase

Something warm and firm rests against my back, and a strong arm holds me close.

Which can only mean I did it. I somehow reached into the cages and pulled out a soul trapped there, something that should be more than impossible.

No wonder I still feel exhausted. The energy required to do such a thing would be astronomical.

Heath's arm tightens around me. "Good morning," he murmurs, lips just an inch from my ear.

"Is it morning?"

"It is for us. Outside of that, I couldn't begin to guess. Nothing makes sense to me down here."

Demonheim isn't really down, and that has more to do with the human's idea of hell than any actual reality. But I don't bother to correct him, understanding that Demonheim is unsettling enough for outsiders.

"What happened when I was out?"

"As you can see, the wolf let me go." He says it so dryly, and I force myself to sit up so I can take him in.

He's right, of course. He's fully a man again, fur and snout and four legs gone. "I think the wolf liked me," I tell him.

"Of course the wolf likes you," Heath says, like it's obvious. "You're it's entire reason for living."

"That might be an exaggeration," I force a chuckle, turning away.

He reaches up to grip my chin, turning my face back to him. "No, it's not. That's the point of a wolf. We're made for our packs and our mates, and the wolf itself only comes out to protect. That wolf would die for you just as quickly as I would, Chase."

"Don't die for me," I say firmly, reaching out to touch the hand holding my face.

Heath sits up, the blanket draping to his waist, leaving his chest bare. He leans towards me, tilting my chin. "Wolves are made to protect our mates. But we don't have to talk about it right now."

"What should we talk about?" I ask, because there're likely dozens of things that need our attention at the moment.

"That can wait," he murmurs, and then leans in to kiss me.

The kiss isn't gentle; it's the result of desperation, of fear, of almost losing each other. Of knowing we are more than lucky to even get this moment together after everything.

And it's everything we need at this moment. He's here. We survived.

Right now, we don't have to think about tomorrow. We don't have to think about Demonheim or my father or our future—we can just be.

Heath ends up on his back, with me leaning over him, the two of us exchanging biting, desperate kisses. I want to consume him. I want everything, every inch of him. I want to know him, inside and out.

And then he reaches up a hand to stroke two fingers along my left horn, and I am gone. Any remaining control is lost, and I collapse on top of him, losing hold on myself, rocking my hips against his.

I'm reminded that the last time we did this, we were interrupted, and I'm desperate to finish what we started.

"If you keep doing that, I might come," I warn him, immediately undercutting the seriousness of my warning by rocking my hips against him, lining my cock up with his, feeling the bulge press against me. My eyes roll back as he touches my horn again.

"If I sucked your horn like it was your cock, what would you do?" Is the only thing he asks.

"Make a mess in my trousers. Speaking of sucking cocks..."

"I wasn't actually speaking of sucking cocks." He smiles as he says it, groping my ass and making me rock my hips harder.

"I want to suck yours."

He hisses, but when I try to find the waistline of his trousers, his hand stops me.

"As much as I want this—and I do, trust me—we have company right outside this room, and I'd rather not do this with an audience."

"Company?" I force myself to sit up. "Who?"

"You remember that I had someone with me in the cages, right?"

To tell the truth, no, I didn't. I'd long since forgotten the specifics. But glowing blue eyes come back to me now.

"And she's outside this room?" I demand, scrambling to free myself from the grabby hands of a warm, heavy-eyed wolf. "You just left her there? For how long?"

"What was I supposed to do with her?"

"I don't know, but you realize she was in the cages." And the cages are only for the worst of the worst. For those beyond saving, beyond rationality. Who knows what we've brought out of there?

Heath goes very quiet for a long moment, then says, "She helped me, when she could have left me to lose my mind. I have to honor that."

I groan. I also feel for whoever this woman in my sitting room is. Whether or not she deserved the cages, we can't argue that they aren't awful. And that might just make it worse. If she's been in there for a while, she's no doubt lost her rationality. We're in the middle of a war. If she gets loose, if she says the wrong thing to any demon, gets seen anywhere she shouldn't be—it's over.

"Besides, she's a demon," Heath continues, oblivious to my plight. "And I thought demons didn't put demons in the cages."

That puts a halt to my racing thoughts. "She's a demon?"

"Horns and all."

"Who?"

"She didn't tell me that."

A demon in the cages. That should not happen. Maybe there is something strange about this woman after all, something worth pulling out of the cages to debate over.

"Find a shirt," I tell him. "We're going to deal with this now."

Heath groans but gets out of bed, picking his shirt off the floor and following me obediently into the other room.

Where I'm immediately stopped in my tracks. Because I recognize the woman sitting on my sofa, looking like she's just waiting patiently for some conversation to continue.

Her dark hair is wild and matted, she's far too thin, and her eyes are vacant. I've never seen her so filthy or poorly dressed; she's typically immaculately put together. Nonetheless, those lightning-blue eyes are unmistakable.

I go to one knee right there, blocking the doorway and bowing my head. "Your majesty," I murmur.

Because sitting before me is Queen Olette, Ryder's mother and rightful queen of all Demonheim, long assumed murdered by her husband.

CHAPTER FIFTEEN

HEATH

I blink at the scene before me. Chase doesn't rise, remaining on one knee, head bowed, waiting for this woman to release him.

His queen, apparently. I study her, trying to see anything queenly in her.

My sister is a queen. She might never look especially polished, she might like to brawl with the rest of us, but there is a presence about her at all times, like the crown is always there, even when she so rarely wears it. It's not something that can be ignored about her.

But this woman, you would never guess her to be a queen. You'd never guess her to be anyone of any consequence.

I watch her and realize she's not aware of what's happening in front of her. Chase remains on his knee, head bowed, but she just hums to herself. "Is there any food?" she asks.

Chase looks up, gaping. "I can get some."

"I'd like that. I haven't been hungry in so long."

Her thin, emaciated frame says otherwise, but I realize I also didn't feel hunger for however long I was in that cage. Most likely the cages suppressed hunger, just like it did every other sensation.

I'm hungry now, I realize belatedly, the clawing sensation persistent now that I've allowed myself to think about it.

"You have to stay here with me," I tell her. "Chase can get us food."

"I... of course," Chase murmurs, moving to stand. I extend a hand to help him up, but he's already on his feet. "Care to move the sofa, Heath?"

I push it away from the door with the woman still on it, then stand between her and the door in case she gets it into her mind to make a run for it. "We'll be waiting for you," I tell Chase, trying to keep my voice pitched just for us. "And when you get back, we'll talk?"

He nods, seeming almost distracted, although I can't really blame him. If this is really the lost demon queen—

I can't even begin to think of what the next steps are. This changes everything.

Why is she alive? Why would her husband risk leaving her alive? I doubt it has anything to do with affection.

"You might have mentioned your name," I tell her.

She just looks at me, long and hard. "There are no names in the cages."

I swallow. True enough. If I'd been alone in there any longer, I know I would have forgotten myself entirely.

How long was I in there, anyway? I need to ask Chase. Has Hannah given up on me yet? Is my family worried about how long I've been gone?

I've been away on projects for longer before, of course, but never without Celia's explicit permission.

If Celia thinks I'm dead, thinks the last thing we did together was argue—I don't want to think about it.

I'm not dead, I remind myself. And between Chase and I and now this lost queen, I won't die, either. We'll come up with a plan and I'll return home to make amends.

And I'll return with my mate in tow, so everyone will forgive me just about anything. A new mate—a new pack member—is worth more than any stupid choices I might have made.

The door re-opening jars me from my thoughts. I tense, ready to leap into action, to do whatever it takes to protect this queen and me. But the scent of apples reaches me, and I relax.

Chase comes bearing food, multiple plates stacked on top of each other. "This will have to last a day or two," he warns. "Taking too much will become too obvious too quickly."

"We'll ration ourselves." He and I will, at any rate. As for the queen... well, who knows what she'll do.

Chase hands her a plate first, bowing his head as he does. "Your Majesty."

She studies him. "Do I know you?"

"My name is Chase," he says. I see him holding entirely still, waiting to see if that leads to any memories.

It doesn't seem to; instead, she simply nods and eats her food, very clearly not worried about rationing.

That's alright. I'll pick at mine a bit and be fine. I'm sure I didn't go that long without food.

Chase is still staring at the queen, but I need an answer to this question, so I interrupt. "How long has it been?"

He turns to me with a stricken look, pain evident in his eyes. I think bringing it up hurts him as much as it does me. "Ten days."

Ten days. Good gods. I shudder.

That was ten days in the cages. What would a month do? A year?

It could be worse, I suppose. No one outside of Demonheim is likely to panic over ten days, so it's unlikely Hannah has sent word to my family. Ten days is recoverable. Ten days is...

Ten days is an awful amount of time to spend on those cages, I think grimly. No matter how long or short, that place is intolerable.

How long has the queen been presumed dead? No wonder she's not all there.

Chase sets the food down and holds my face, directing me to look at him. "Are you okay?" When I don't answer right away, he winces. "Stupid question."

It isn't, though. Because just that simple touch from him makes me feel, if not okay, at least more grounded in the present moment.

"Have you ever been in the cages before I called you there?" I ask.

"No. No demon goes in there."

Except now, there have been two.

"It's the absence that gets to me," I explain. "There is nothing there. Nothing. And now every little thing, it's like it's too much. Every color, every scent. Every sound makes me twitch."

The world is too big, I've suddenly realized, even though I've been confined to a relatively small suite of rooms. There is simply too much, the difference between nothing and everything too jarring.

Before, it hadn't been a problem. I had my mate to focus on, after all. Chase falling unconscious, looking for all the world like what I'd asked of him had killed him—that had been enough of a distraction to shift my focus.

But I've been in enough battles to know that there is only so long that you can ignore the problem. A good soldier can ignore discomfort to get the job done, but eventually, it will catch up to them. There's no way around it.

For me, that eventually just happens to be now.

It shouldn't be. I still have a coup to organize, after all, and the queen presents a new variable to consider. I should be able to focus, to channel everything into my goal.

But I find that I can only partially do so. Some part of my mind—an ever-growing part—is entirely consumed by what happened in the cages.

Chase's hand on my face turns to a gentle stroke. "What can I do?"

I close my eyes. I want nothing more than to stare into his face, but it's too much.

I'm scared that if I allow myself to have it, I'll say what I need.

I need him to hold me. To bring me to bed and hold me tight. To let the only sensations in this overwhelming world be him, just for a little while.

But that's not an option. We have other things to be concerned about, starting with the queen, who will always be in the next room, and ending with the war right outside our door. I can't take time out to hold my mate.

Chase tilts my face towards him again, staring me in the eyes. "I'm going to find the queen a place to rest," he says after a long moment. The corner of his mouth twitches, a small smirk, there and gone. "It would be disrespectful to expect her majesty to sleep on the couch, after all."

"Where?" I ask roughly. "She's not fully rational, Chase, and I don't know if she ever will be, after that. She keeps asking for her mate."

Chase's expression twists. "Her mate is long since dead."

"Right, and she only seems to remember that sometimes. How long has she been in there?"

Chase shrugs. "If she's been in there since the last time any of us saw her, then almost four years."

Four years. It's truly, entirely unimaginable. I want to throw up.

"Do you think she can recover from that?"

"I don't know," he says slowly, clearly mulling it over. "It's never happened before. We've never pulled people out. That's not the point of the cages, after all."

"My point exactly. We can't trust her to look out for her own best interests," I explain to him, daring a quick glance at the woman, who seems for all the world to have no idea we are even in the room with her. She barely seems alive, except for those glowing eyes staring nearly unblinkingly. "If she goes wandering away, looking for her mate, not aware of what's happened, then..."

Then it's over. If the king finds out exactly who we have, then I have no doubt he'll kill her and then us shortly after.

I don't know how the discovery of the queen's survival factors into Ryder's claim for the throne. Perhaps we're talking about an entirely different war now. But either way, I do know we have to protect her. Even from herself.

Chase looks conflicted for a moment, but then nods resolutely, like we just came to some sort of agreement when I don't remember participating in the discussion at all. He turns his head away from me, although I notice he doesn't step any further away. Maybe he's as reluctant as I am to have any distance between us now.

Or maybe he's just worried that I am as unstable as the queen and wants to be here to keep me in check if it's necessary.

"Your majesty," he says. His voice is a soothing, calm mixture that I haven't heard him use yet. It sounds like the voice one might use for a beloved child, or perhaps a pet that needs extra coddling. "How would you feel about getting some rest?"

Well, if he's about to give her his bedroom, I suppose that will firmly quash any silly fantasies I have about lying in bed together.

But then he walks over to a seemingly blank wall and puts his hand on it, scrunching together his face like he's thinking of something incredibly complicated. When he moves his hand back, a large wooden door appears.

He pushes the door open, revealing a second bedroom and a shaking hand. "What do you think, your majesty?" he asks. "Does the room meet your expectations?"

She blinks, seeming to realize that Chase was talking to her, and moves on shaking legs to go see the room he's gesturing her to.

It's a fairly typical bedroom, with a large, well-appointed four poster, soft rugs, and even a filled bath in one corner. "How'd you do that?" I ask, eyeing his shaking hand. "Was that here the entire time?"

"In a manner of speaking," Chase murmurs. "It's the magic of Demonheim. If we feed it, it will give it back to us tenfold. This is our home, after all." He looks at his own shaking hand, then frowns. "It would have worked easier for the queen, but I'm not sure she could focus enough to do it right now."

Probably a fair assumption, I think grimly. "Will you be okay?"

"Right as rain, soon," he promises. He turns back to the queen. "Is it enough, your majesty?"

"Will my love be joining me soon?"

We both stand in silence, not willing to lie to her, not ready to tell her the truth. Thankfully, she seems to distract herself quite nicely, exploring the room until she reaches the bath, where she begins to unlace her clothes.

Chase shuts the door immediately, leaning against it like he thinks she's going to force it open and make us watch her disrobe. "I think she's satisfied," he murmurs. "We should block the main door again."

I move the couch back in place, and add Chase's desk, too, for good measure.

When I'm done, Chase snakes his arms around me from behind. "Now that that's settled..."

Chapter Sixteen

Chase

I should have been aware sooner that Heath is falling apart.

The man is my mate. My mate, who I should always be aware of, who I should know without thinking. His moods and feelings should be second-nature to me.

Maybe this will help. After all, we haven't had much time together, and he did just spend ten days in the cages. Things are bound to be a little difficult.

Today will fix things.

"Come join me in bed." It sounds more like an order than an offer, I realize, and I try to rephrase it immediately. "Please. We could both... for both of us."

Heath actually shudders in my grip, but then he nods. Too quickly, I think, like he's desperate for this, like he was just waiting for it to be brought up.

"Come on," I murmur, as gently as I can. I take his hand, and he wraps his big fingers around my still shaking ones. Immediately, the contact with him helps.

I tug gently, leading up both back to my bedroom. Then, without a word, I pull off his clothes. When I'm done, I push him onto the bed, then take off my clothes. All I want is skin-on-skin, the two of us feeling nothing but each other and the blanket wrapped around us.

I lie on the bed next to Heath, our clothes in a pile on the floor, and pull him into my arms. He shudders at the contact, then buries his head in my chest.

I close my eyes, then stroke over his hair, stunned by how easily he goes soft and limp under my touch, stunned by how badly he apparently needed this.

His hair is soft as silk under my touch, and every stroke relaxes me, simultaneously replenishing the magic I spent and just soothing the worry that's hung over me like a sword for the past ten days. For the past several years, really.

Perhaps Heath isn't the only one who needs this tonight.

"What else do you need?" I ask, doing my best to keep my voice soft, hoping not to startle him.

He's silent for a long moment, so long that I begin to suspect he won't answer. "Nothing," he eventually says. "Just this. Just keep doing this."

I dare to press a kiss to the crown of his head. "Whenever you need it," I promise. "Always."

We don't say anything else, just letting Heath bask in the quiet, tight hug, and me bask in having my mate in my arms.

***

Somewhere in there, we must fall asleep, because I wake up with a mouthful of Heath's soft hair nearly choking me. At some point in the night, he'd drifted impossibly closer, lying entirely on top of me.

Heath is a big man, built like a tree, but I don't feel like I'm crushed underneath him. I feel surrounded by him, my skin tingling everywhere he touches me.

Some of that is the energy, the little jolt we demons get from contact with our mates. But some of it is all him, I think, a spark because there is an incredibly attractive man surrounding me.

I plan to wake up this way every day for the rest of my hopefully very long life. It doesn't matter if we're here in Demonheim or Ryder's war camp or wherever Heath comes from or anywhere else. We're never sleeping apart again.

Heath wakes up, immediately burying his face in the crook of my neck. "You smell so good in the mornings," he mumbles. "All sleepy and slow."

I almost ask him what sleepy smells like, but I already know I'll get an answer that will make just as much sense as my explanation of the energy from a mating bond will for him. So instead, I ask, "Do I not smell good at other times?"

"You smell perfect," he says, dragging his nose down to my chest. I don't know if it's for exaggerated affect, meant to be a seductive gesture, or if he really is just lost in my scent. Either way, I like it. There's something especially alluring about being the center of Heath's attention, and it makes me go soft and pliant beneath him. "Always." He looks up at me with a heartbreakingly sweet smile. "Like apples. I chased that scent through Demonheim. When I could finally sense anything again, it was your scent that made me feel safe."

My throat feels swollen, and it takes me a second to find the words. "I'm glad I make you feel safe, Heath. You make me feel safe, too."

"Because I've done such a good job of making you safe," he mumbles, turning his face away from me.

I squeeze him. "You went into the cages to save me. I won't forget that." He shudders when I just say the words. "Do you want to talk about it?"

"No," he says, but it sounds petulant, and I resist the urge to laugh, just waiting him out.

It's incredibly disarming to feel like you've known someone your whole life because you care about them so much, because every drop of blood in your body sings for them, but at the same time know next to nothing about them.

We need to rectify that, I think grimly. I won't live in a world where there's an inch of space between Heath and me, not even in our minds.

"You don't understand," he says after a long minute.

"Probably not, but I'd like to."

"Wolves don't have magic. We're not even supposed to turn into wolves. But what we do have is our senses. I can smell the emotions of an enemy across a battlefield, can hear across a forest. And when I was cut off from that..." He shudders. "A part of me was missing. And I don't know how to survive without that part."

"You'll never have to again," I promise, and I mean it. I will do anything to stop Heath from ever being back in those cages.

He doesn't answer, just re-burying his face in my neck, taking a deep, deep draw of air. It tickles, but I fight not to move.

This is exactly what both of us need.

***

I don't bother to keep track of the hours, unworried and unhurried. There's a thought at the back of my mind, the reminder of the larger picture, of Ryder and Hannah and my father and the battle for the control of Demonheim. But I force those thoughts out of my head, focused entirely on my mate. Heath, here and now, has to be my priority.

Yet at some point, he sits up in bed, letting the blanket fall to pool around his hips. He sits, knees drawn up, watching me, and I reach out a hand, trying to continue to give him the contact he was so desperately craving earlier.

"We need to talk about the plan," he says, his voice still heavy, but somehow sounding more present than earlier.

"Only if you're ready," I tell him.

He barks out a laugh. "I don't know when I'll be ready, Chase, but this isn't the type of thing we can ignore indefinitely. For one thing, what do we do about your queen? Does she change things?"

I wince at the very thought. "I don't know. By rights, the throne is hers, but—"

"But she's not especially lucid."

"Maybe she can be again. She's been in the cages for four years, we've barely given her time to recover, and—"

"Can Demonheim wait for her to recover?" he asks pointedly. The question is harsh, but the tone isn't. Heath doesn't mean it to be cruel, or disparaging of the queen. To him, this is just a fact.

I remember the queen on the throne, of course. I remember her rule, fair and just. A little muddled in the last years, but everyone is willing to extend grace and understanding after the loss of a demon's mate.

And my father had trampled all over that, slipping in like a snake, and none of us knew until it was far too late.

"I keep wondering why she's alive," Heath continues. "Did the king hate her so much that he chose to punish her with the cages over the certainty of killing her? I know escaping the cages is rare—"

"—Impossible—" I interrupt.

"—Rare," he emphasizes, "But still. He had to know killing her would be more certain." He says it with a clinical detachment, but he winces at the end, as if hearing his own words.

I can't blame him, though; I puzzled over the very same thing. "Demonheim is a powerful entity," I say, sharing my best guess. "And while the power that feeds it comes through all demons, there's one demon that's the conduit. The one most able to master that power. Naturally, that's our ruler. And if Queen Olette died—I think the king realized the power would just pass to his son. Naturally, something he never wanted."

"So keeping her alive but incapacitated was a matter of practicality," Heath concludes. "A way of holding onto power."

"Holding onto some power. That sword of his helps people believe he's more powerful than he is. He is powerful, but he's no royal. If you saw the queen on the throne... and her son will be like her, I imagine. Either one of them would destroy him in moments, if they were on the throne of Demonheim once more."

"Is that a literal statement? Do we just need to get them literally on the throne?"

"It's more complicated than that—otherwise, any idiot who sits on the throne would take over, and we'd have a regime change every other day. But if one has the power, and sits on the throne, then yes. As far as I know, that's it."

"You said the king doesn't have the power."

"Between his wife's—probably inadvertent—blessing and the sword, he was considered enough. You have to know how much demons like bending rules. I imagine he spent years plotting, digging through every scrap of information he could find, ensuring his little coup d'etat would hold."

"So if we could get the queen physically on the throne...?" he asks.

"It may be enough. But you weren't wrong: is she in any fit state to do it?"

Heath shrugs, something about his eyes saying he's miles beyond that thought now. "Who cares? No one says it has to be permanent. If her son comes in after and takes her place, then that's fine. But she'll be an improvement on the current ruler, at least."

"I'm not so worried about her ability to rule, although that does concern me," I admit. "I mean, getting her to the throne won't be easy. It might be bloody, and will require her to follow instructions so she doesn't get killed or give away our plan. Do you think she can?"

That gets him to pause a moment, looking troubled. "Maybe if we give her a little time, she'll come back enough," he says, but I can hear the doubt. "Like you said, it's been four years. And I have my mate to support me, and she thinks hers is alive half the time and is devastated she can't find him. But maybe a few days? I'm not expecting perfection, but a little more lucidity would make all the difference."

I want to argue that a few days means a few more days of my father doing awful things. But he's fully aware, and he's not wrong.

We need a plan with the best chance of success, and if that means waiting a few days longer, then that's what we'll do.

"And if she doesn't become more lucid?" I dare to ask, hating to think about it. She's my queen, she's my queen and I can feel it in my bones, and thinking badly of her feels wrong. But it's also a very real possibility.

"We cross that bridge if we come to it," he says.

I study him for a moment, trying to see where his head is at. I see his mind turning, trying to delve deeper into the problem of what we should do.

He's the same Heath I held last night until we both slept, the same Heath I desperately tried to keep grounded in the here-and-now, into a world that I have to remind him is still real.

I see my mate, in need of me once more, and I set the plans for the future, for the war, aside. It's instinctual, the mating bond taking over, pushing me to give him what he needs. What we both need.

I sit up, sliding my arms around his shoulders, letting my hand trail over a well-developed pectoral muscle. "In the meantime..." I murmur, right next to his ear, letting the words hang out there like an offer, waiting to see if he'll take it.

Chapter Seventeen

Heath

"In the meantime..." he offers, voice a seductive rasp in my ear, and I suddenly understand how demon deals get done. Who could possibly ever resist that voice?

Chase could trade my life for garbage, and in that voice, I think I'd blindly agree. I'd give him anything he asked for, follow any plan, if it meant he would speak to me like that again.

His hand teases over my chest, finding my nipple on its third or fourth pass. I shudder when he lightly brushes it. He pauses for a moment, then does it again, more deliberately, before passing back over and tweaking the nipple gently.

Gods above, this man is determined to remind me of what it means to be back in the real world. And I'm eagerly going to follow wherever he leads.

"In the meantime?" I ask him, playing dumb, making him spell it out just to hear his voice again.

"We've made a lot of promises already," he says, his voice barely a breath tickling over my ear. "And we've been interrupted too many times. I believe I was about to suck your cock when we got interrupted, hm?"

My cock is certainly very interested in that, already plumping up without a single touch yet. "And do you plan to revisit that moment?"

He leans in and nips at my ear, sharp teeth making all my breath leave my body for a moment. "What better way to give you some real, undeniable sensations, right?"

"No arguments from me." I couldn't come up with a single damn argument now if I tried.

"Sit on the edge of the bed for me," he murmurs, and I hasten to obey.

The king of Demonheim himself could burst into this room, sword aloft, and I wouldn't be able to focus on anything but Chase sliding to his knees on the floor, looking up at me from between my spread thighs.

I can't resist; I reach down and lightly grasp each horn, stroking my thumb over the hard points. He shudders. "Careful there," he murmurs. "Distract me too much and we won't get anywhere."

"I want to see you come from your horns being played with again, so that's not a deterrent."

He leans in and bites at my thigh, leaving a red mark behind that will probably last a few hours. "I've been waiting to suck your cock, Heath. You won't take this away from me."

And that is a very compelling argument. I obediently take my hands off his horns, but I leave one hand in his hair, letting the light waves fall through my fingers.

I open my mouth to ask him if he has any rules, if he has anything I should avoid—I like being a considerate lover—but then he kisses the crown of my aching cock, and all words escape me.

All language escapes me. I let out a wordless moan that only increases in volume when he slides his lips down, engulfing the head of my cock, sucking gently as his tongue teases me.

Fuck me. Nothing in my life has ever felt this good. Chase's mouth owns me, body and soul, as he attempts to suck my brain out through my cock.

He might be succeeding, too, with a particularly skilled bob of his head, taking me deeper and deeper into him, until I'm surrounded by the tight, welcoming heat of his throat.

"Fuck, Chase, you—" I gasp, unable to finish my thought.

His hands slide up my thighs, a sensual caress he uses to push them even wider open, giving himself just a little more room.

Then, with a particularly skilled swipe of his tongue, I come, unable to resist grabbing at his hair, bucking my hips towards his face, desperately chasing what he's promising with lips and tongue. And gods above, does he deliver.

He swallows every drop, even making a show of licking his lips when he pops off of my cock, and if I wasn't already boneless from my orgasm, my cock might stir in interest at the sight.

"Worth the wait," Chase decrees after a moment. "And something I'm doing every day for the rest of our lives."

"You plan to kill me, then," I say weakly.

Chase chuckles, dark and menacing, and that, paired with the sensual whisper from earlier, tells me everything I need to know about the demon I've more than welcomed into my life.

Wolves are sensual creatures. We're obsessed with scent, with taste, with sloppy, raw sex. We're obsessed with each sound and sight of pleasure we can wring from our mates. Hell, we're just obsessed with sex, considering that nature gave us the compulsive need to rut on the full moon.

Chase is sensual too, in a slower, more refined way. He likes making me squirm. He'll probably like making me beg. And I am fucking obsessed with it already.

Chase crawls up into my lap, knees on either side of my thighs. His cock, hard and leaking, hits my stomach, and I bite my lip, considering if I can flip him onto the bed and suck his cock, or if I want to try to get him off with just his horns again.

"You said you needed sensation to feel real," he points out, winding his arms around my neck, stroking his fingers through the hair at the nape of my neck.

And well, he's more than right about that. I never expected him to deliver in such a spectacular way, but I'd be a liar if I said it didn't work.

Chapter Eighteen

Chase

Heath's lazy-eyed, contented stare makes me burn for him.

I've never been this hard in my life. My cock is leaking pre-come between us, and my balls already ache, desperate for relief.

And my skin positively vibrates where we touch, like his skin is made of lightning.

I've heard for years about the power in the energy from a mate, but this is truly beyond my wildest expectations. Demon deals will forever feel dirty after a single touch from my mate.

"Tell me how I can take care of you," I tell him, playing absently with his hair. "What do you need, Heath?"

He laughs disbelievingly. "I think you've done a fine job of taking care of me, Chase."

Maybe, but it's just a start. "Tell me what you like," I press. "Let me touch you, Heath. Let me make you come."

"Again?" he asks, eyebrow raised. "Is once not enough?"

I lean in to whisper in his ear, like what I have to say is a secret, even if we're the only two around to hear. Still, he shivers exactly like I thought he would when my lips touch his ear, and I grin as I begin to speak. "Every time you touch me, I get stronger. But the energy when you came..." I nip his ear. "You have no idea."

"So I'm a power source for you?"

"I also just really like watching you come," I say, deciding now is not the time to attempt to explain demon magic to him. I pull back so I can look at him, smiling. "So, what'll it be?"

"Will you fuck me?" he asks me, eyes steady on mine as he asks. "Make me feel real, Chase."

It would be an absolute honor. Make me feel real. Of course. Whatever I can do. "How do you like it?" I ask, one hand absently trailing over his chest, considering my options.

He swallows, and I watch his throat bob. "Hard and fast. Something I'll feel."

I consider it for a moment, but then shake my head. "No, I don't think so."

I worry he'll get upset, but he just looks amused. "Why bother to ask, then?"

"I thought you might have good ideas, but clearly your desperation has addled your brain," I tease.

"Oh? Do tell." He's certainly amused, and it fills me with a giddy feeling, a soft, bubbly joy to see him like this.

"You want to feel something? Hard and fast isn't the only way to get there. More to the point, fast will be fast. No, I think you need slow. Deep. Teasing."

His throat bobs again. "I could be convinced."

I'm sure he can. And I'm the man for the job. Heath doesn't know it yet, but I have every intention of showing him exactly how much I can make him feel.

I palm my own cock, the move blatant enough that Heath watches, licking his lips. The challenge of this will be holding off long enough to make Heath react the way I want him to. After all, he's already come once, while I've just been dreaming about it since he made me come the day we met.

"I think I'll like convincing you of things," I tell him.

"Do you plan to make it a regular habit?"

"That depends—will you always give in?"

His eyes dart to my cock for a moment, then trail back up my body slowly, settling on my mouth for a moment before returning to my eyes. "Probably."

Yes, probably—from what I know, that would indeed be expected from a mated wolf. So I give him a truth back. "I think you could turn the tables and it would work the same," I confess. "But not today. Today, I'll convince you."

I think this man could look at me with those languid, sex-filled golden eyes, and I'd give him anything he asks for. I think if he crooks his fingers just so, I'd walk through flames to follow him.

I think we both know it. Maybe that's what made fate choose us for the mating bond: the fact that we'd both give this to each other.

"Are you comfortable with me at your back?" I ask him, moving to stand again.

He reaches for me, seemingly unconscious of the move, and I'm gratified to know he hates extra space between us as much as I do. But he nods, moving so he's on his front, weight supported on his elbows, his beautiful ass presented to me. Toned, firm, and the same even tan as the rest of him, the sight is so mesmerizing that I almost miss his explanation that, with my scent, he'd know me anywhere.

My hands come down to frame his ass, thumbs stroking over the meat of it as I squeeze lightly. The flesh barely gives under my hands.

I teased him about going slow; I promised I'd make him feel this. I need to keep my promise, but it's getting more difficult, just staring at this perfection in front of me.

I take one hand off his ass to palm myself, attempting to take some of the edge off. It's largely unsuccessful, just driving me to want him more.

The gods have presented me with a true wonder of a mate, and now they're just making sure I know it.

Like I could ever forget it.

Deciding to test the magical energy supposedly given to us by our mates in a way slightly less intense than transporting souls out of the damn cages, I close my eyes and summon a vial of oil. After a second, the cold, solid bottle appears in my hands.

I open my eyes to stare at it. Even that seemingly small object should have drained my energy a bit unless I drew from some sort of deal with someone else. Bending the rules of nature always has a cost.

But I don't feel any loss of energy. I feel a slight tingling under my skin, a permanent reminder of my mate's presence.

I swallow and firmly set aside any thoughts of demon magic, any thoughts of how the mating bond firmly blows apart all the rules of magic and existence I'd known for centuries now. There will be time for that later.

Now, I have the oil, and a warm, tempting ass in front of me, and a mate who's desperate to feel.

"Spread your thighs a bit for me," I tell him. He does as I ask, giving me room to slide in closer. "Can I use my fingers on you?"

"You can do whatever you want," Heath says, his voice growing huskier. "Just—please."

I uncork the bottle and apply the liquid to my fingers, rubbing for just a second to warm it against my preternaturally hot skin. Then I use the thumb on my free hand to reveal his hole to me.

Gods, he's beautiful. I have half a mind to abandon the thought of fingering him and instead taste him again, but have to quickly discard it. As good a game as I talked about slow and deep, giving him the sensation he really craves, I can't hold out forever. I need to be inside of him.

He shivers delightfully when I touch him, just the lightest, teasing touch. "Feeling yet?" I ask him.

"Shut up," he says, but the word is half swallowed by a moan, so I presume he doesn't truly mean it.

I sink one finger inside him, feeling the tight heat of him, this gods-blessed space that I'm now obsessed with.

"Chase, I—" he cuts himself off with another moan, so I wait patiently, finger still inside him. "Give me more."

"Hm. No."

He bucks his hips, the movement a combination of demand and protest. "No?"

"No," I tell him again, trying to hide my smile even though he's facing away from me. "You asked to feel something. You asked me to make you feel something. Have you changed your mind?"

"I will if you're going to take all night to get to it," he grumbles, but he rocks his hips experimentally again.

I chuckle. "I'll take all night if I want. And you'll love every minute of it." To emphasize it, I give him another finger, sliding it in alongside the first, gratified by his deep moan.

Gods, what a beautiful man.

When he's rocking back into my hand, when I think I've truly made him desperate, when he's soft and giving under my touch, I lean down and pepper kisses up his back, starting at the base of his spine and slowly working my way up his spine, over his shoulder blades, then up his neck. Finally, I stop at his ear, teasing the lobe with my teeth before saying, "Are you ready for me?"

"You know I am," he says, his voice gratifyingly breathless now. "Please, Chase."

That's what I want to hear. I nip hard at his earlobe, then kneel upright, removing my fingers so I can grip my cock and feed it into him.

CHAPTER NINETEEN

HEATH

Gods above, Chase is determined to kill me. The cages didn't, six hundred years of various battles didn't, but this one man, this one very determined demon, will.

What a way to go.

He fills me slowly, like he has to make it last just that much longer, torment me just that much more. I feel every inch of his cock entering me, the sweet, aching pressure of it.

When exactly did I last get fucked? I can't even think about it right now, couldn't summon a date if my life depended on it. There's only here, and now, and Chase, now fully seated inside me, stretching me open around him.

He holds perfectly still, frozen in place, likely giving me time to adjust. It's time I don't want, don't need—the slight burn is exactly what I'm after.

But maybe he's just continuing on his quest to make me as wild as possible, to draw this out as long as he can. The man has turned fucking into a sweet, sweet art of torture.

I rock back against him. "Fuck me, Chase," I murmur. "Show me what you can do."

He seems happy to oblige, pulling nearly entirely out of me before thrusting in again, the time for the slow, teasing build seemingly over.

It's so good, punching the air out of my lungs as he fills me with deep, steady thrusts. I groan and rock into it, letting his movements wash away everything else. It's just this. Just us, here and now, his cock stroking inside me, his hands gripping my hips.

Just this. Nothing else exists, nothing else matters, and I can just—

"Oh," I gasp. It comes out a breathless mewl, more sound than word, as he finds the exact right angle to make me see stars.

"There?" he asks, squeezing my hip. The question seems to be rhetorical, because he keeps going, not breaking pace, now hitting that spot on every thrust.

I shift so my left elbow is supporting my weight, leaving my right hand free to find my cock. Chase might've had ideas of this lasting all night long, but quite frankly I think I deserve credit for lasting this long, with my blood singing, with my mate pumping inside me.

Chase doesn't stop me, only makes a hum of approval and arousal as I find my own cock, stroking myself as Chase uses his hands on my hips to pull me even further back onto his cock.

"Are you close?" he asks me.

I nod frantically, words long since gone.

"Me too," he says. "But I want to see you come first, Heath. I bet it's beautiful, so—please. Show me."

I think it's the *please* that does it, that soft little plea, the idea that Chase wants this badly enough to ask. Wants me badly enough. I can't stop myself. I come, groaning Chase's name as my seed coats my hand, my stomach, and the bed.

Chase continues to rock inside me, one, two, three, four more pumps, then he too is coming, a shout hanging on the air as he spills inside me.

We're both panting there for a moment, getting our breath back as we come down from that high.

Then Chase pulls out of me, leaving nothing but a sticky openness behind. He tugs at me until I'm laying with him, our bodies entirely pressed against each other, and kisses me. It's a soft kiss, a gentle kiss, a hint of a promise between us.

And, lying there, freshly fucked, dripping come, slightly sore, and in the arms of my mate, I feel more solid than I have since coming out of the cages.

Chapter Twenty

Chase

We wake up sticky, but neither of us complains about it.

If anything, Heath just snuggles deeper into me, and my heart goes soft. I never knew I could be this soft, this gentle. Like I could become one of the people who sees the world as sugar-spun, as sunshine days and happy moments.

But here I am, holding Heath for a moment longer, waiting to mention what waits ahead of us.

Heath breaks the silence first. "We need to check on the queen," he says.

I pull back far enough to look at him and see him watching me back, seemingly steady. His eyes seem sharper than they have since the cages, his look serious but not anxious.

So I nod. "Who gets to bathe while the other checks on her?"

He raises an eyebrow. "I have come inside me still. So."

"I have the magic to make the tub fill. So."

We stare at each other for a moment, then Heath cracks a smile first. "And what kind of demon deal would I need to convince you to use that magic for my benefit?"

I pretend to consider it. "We seal deals with a kiss, you know," I say.

It's his turn to pretend to think. "I think I could pay with that."

Then he knocks me onto my back, kissing me stupid, biting his way into my mouth.

"Payment enough?" he teases, his breath fanning against my jaw.

He's playing, but I don't think he understands how true it is. A kiss from my mate genuinely is as much energy as I'd get from binding some poor human to my will. What I'd have to trick and steal from another, always leaving them a little less, is freely given here.

I snap my fingers and the tub in the corner fills with clean, hot water.

"When you're done, you're going to have to explain how that works," he murmurs, smiling, already trying to evade my grabbing hands to slide out of bed. I can't help but try to grab him, though; Heath's smile is the most magical thing I've ever seen.

"Non-demons never get demon magic. Don't worry about it."

He stops moving and turns to look at me, eyes serious. "Chase, if we're going to spend the rest of our hopefully very long lives together, I'm at least going to try to understand. So you can explain it to me. As many times as it takes."

He looks so determined that I don't argue. "Once I check on her," I agree, allowing him to leave the bed so I can get up too, hunting for my trousers from last night. I wince as I slide them on, but decidedly don't complain. Heath is right about deserving the first bath.

Once we finish this war, once we seat Ryder on the throne, can we find a place with a bath big enough for two?

I forcibly turn away from my mate and leave our bedroom.

The door to the queen's room is still shut. I lay my hand against the wood, and Demonheim informs me it hasn't been opened.

Demonheim likes me, but I know without a doubt that it likes the queen better. It would lie on her behalf, even to me, if she asked it to. So, with an uneasy feeling, I knock.

The door opens a moment later, seemingly of its own volition, and I wince. That type of magic, that type of manipulation of Demonheim's magic, might have been an afterthought when she was queen and had full command of the realm. Was it still? Or did my father's coup diminish her power?

Does she even know the difference? Is she rational enough to remember what happened?

She's sitting on the edge of the bed. Her filthy clothes are gone, replaced by clothes that fit her poorly but at least are clean. I wonder where she managed to get them, but then consider if they are a gift from the realm. If they were already hers, and that's why they fit so poorly.

She's wasted away to nearly nothing in these past four years.

"Your majesty," I say, breaking the silence. She looks at me, those bright eyes unnervingly piercing into me, but I have a feeling she's only half focused. "Do you need anything?"

"Have you seen my mate?" she asks.

Her mate has been dead for decades now. I swallow. "I'm sorry, your majesty," but then I stop there. How do I explain it to her?

Why is it my duty to explain it to her? And would she even remember if I did?

"Do you need food?" I ask instead. It's a coward's response, but it's all I have.

She doesn't answer for a long moment. "He's dead, isn't he?"

I nod slowly, not knowing what to say. "For a while now. Yes."

She doesn't look at me. "Was it my fault?"

"No, your majesty," I say firmly. "You didn't do anything wrong." Her mate's brother being a homicidal throne-stealer who manipulated her in her grief can hardly be classified as her fault. "It's not your fault. And he wouldn't want you to think it was, either."

That's a bold claim, but I make it anyway. I didn't know her mate particularly well—it's not like my father acknowledged me, so we never associated as family—so I shouldn't speak for him. But I think of Heath, and what I'd want someone to say to him if I was gone.

She nods, a slow, uncertain movement, and her eyes become unfocused again.

I let the silence hang heavy between us for another moment. "Would you like some food?" I ask again.

She sighs. "Please."

I leave before I have to figure out if she remembers the conversation we just had a moment ago.

***

I'd prefer not to go out. Every time I step foot out of this room, I risk getting dragged into something. Someone might finally put the pieces together and realize that me being the sole survivor of the portal and being the one to detain Heath is suspicious. Or I might just get called to my father's presence, since he thinks I'm so loyal, and I don't know how to handle facing him now.

Unfortunately, going out seems unavoidable. I can't simply steal a pile of food, not without drawing too much unwanted attention. So I'll have to continuously go out and take it in fits and starts, at least until we're ready for whatever comes next.

Luck, it seems, is not on my side today, because despite my best attempts to avoid crowds, I run into Fariq as I'm pilfering bread rolls from the kitchen.

He eyes me coolly. "Hungry?"

I watch him carefully, trying to feel out if he knows anything he shouldn't. His eyes watch me, unblinking. "Starving," I tell him. "I was up all night reading."

I realize belatedly that, having not tried for a bath before leaving my room, he's likely very aware I was not reading.

It's immaterial. If he's truly worried, let him spend a few days trying to ascertain who my lover is. Let him chase through every demon in Demonheim. I've been with more than a few, and that might bog him down enough to keep him away from me for a day or two.

"Indeed," he says, lip curled. "Anything interesting, Chase? I'm sure your reading is about our portal problem, yes?"

I try to muster a smile, shoving yet another bread roll into my pile. "I'll let you know," I say, and then leave before he can ask any further questions.

Chapter Twenty-One

Heath

The bath stays warm far longer than any normal bath would. Demon magic is apparently quite useful.

I relax into it, letting the hot water soothe the muscles I haven't used in too long, letting it wash away the evidence from our night together.

Chase. My mate. Just the thought of him sends my heart racing.

Considering I came twice last night, I'm not sure how I am more than ready to go again, but here I am, hardening under the water at just the idea of touching Chase again.

Just when I'm debating whether I should take care of it myself, the door reopens.

I'm gratified to see that it's my mate and not the queen. "Are you going to throw me out of the bath?" I ask teasingly, reclining further back in the tub. "Determined it's your turn?"

"You've been soaking there the better part of an hour; your fingers will rot right off," Chase says, already sliding his clothes back off.

I look at my hand, soft and wrinkled by now. "Can't have that," I agree. "I haven't gotten to show you how particularly skilled I am with these yet."

Chase almost trips stepping out of his trousers. "I look forward to it," he says as he recovers.

I use both hands on the rim of the tub to push myself to stand, letting the water sluice off me. Chase comes to a stop again, watching me.

"All yours," I say, looking down at the water as I step out. "Although you might want to magic up fresh water." There had been enough filth on me to truly make the water disgusting.

"Kiss me," he says, voice growing husky, his eyes never leaving my body.

It's an order I'm happy to obey, soaking him with my still-dripping form as I grab him close.

When I move back, he grins at me, then snaps his fingers and the tub refills, water now perfectly clean.

"How do you do that?" I ask, and I know the marvel is clear in my voice. I don't try to hide it; Chase deserves to hear how impressive I find him.

How many buckets of water is that? Sure, I could carry that many buckets. Strength isn't the issue. But the time...

He shrugs, slipping into the water and sighing as the hot water engulfs him. "Demon magic. I just do."

"That's not an answer." I sit on his bed, still completely naked, and watch him, waiting for more.

The room is warm enough that being naked and wet isn't uncomfortable, so I purposefully sprawl out, spreading my legs slightly.

He stares at me for a moment, but evidently decides it's worth explaining this to me after all. Which is smart, because he'll soon find that I'm very persistent.

"Demon magic is all about bending rules," he says at last. "There's nothing saying there *couldn't* be water here. There wasn't, but nothing says it's impossible. So I just bent the rules, and made the water be there."

"That makes very little sense," I confess. What rules? No one makes rules saying where water can and cannot be. Water simply is.

"Well, there you have it. Why outsiders can never take our realm. They never understand the magic that fuels it. We're very good rule-benders, us demons. If we want to be somewhere else in the known world, we can. It would be possible for us to be there, so with the right magic, we can be. And we can fill tubs, and make piles of wealth, and so on."

"But surely it's not that simple," I protest, already thinking of the thousand ways that could be abused, of the nearly unstoppable power that would give someone.

Chase could have ended this war himself if that was the case.

But then again, the king likely would have eliminated all competition, and just thinking this through makes my head ache.

Chase smiles. "Yes, alright. You're catching on. It's all about energy; you can break any rules you want, but it has a cost."

"And the cost is energy?"

He nods. "If you're going to bend the rules of nature, time, and space, you have to pay for it with the energy to make such things possible."

"What is energy, exactly?"

"Exactly what you think it is. It's what makes you function. Small things will make me a little lightheaded, or perhaps make me sleepy. A larger task might literally drain into my life force."

"And filling a tub is...?" I ask, trying to determine where it would fall on this scale.

"That depends. If I'm simply moving water that I already know where it is, then that's less than just casting out into the universe to fill the tub in its entirety."

"Was there water nearby when you filled it, then?"

"Not that I know of."

"So, how much energy did it take?" I ask again.

"Somewhere moderate on that scale, I assume."

I suck in a breath. "That feels like a foolish waste of your energy then."

"Ah, but nothing says it has to be my energy. Why do you think demons make deals? It's a bargain. The deal-maker gives us some energy, and we in turn use that energy for whatever service they're trading for. And there's always a little extra energy on the side."

"So you're siphoning energy from some poor human?"

"It doesn't have to be a human," he corrects me.

"Are any of our kind stupid enough to take those bargains?"

"You'd be surprised. If they need something badly enough, or know the demon well enough, and the cost isn't too high, it happens. But no, I don't siphon energy from humans, to answer your original question."

"Where are you getting enough energy to throw it around like this, then?" I ask, gesturing at the tub.

"You."

"Me?" I ask. "Did I accidentally stumble into a demon deal and not know it?" I should likely be worried, but I can't make myself be. Not when Chase is smiling languidly at me from the tub.

"I mean, calling my name when you were in the cages is a primitive form of a demon bargain—calling my name will always open a door between us. But no, no other deals that I know of."

Well, that's a relief.

I make a mental note about the name. I can foresee a lot of times where I'd want to be able to open that door between us.

"There's a reason demons have mates," he continues. "It's like free energy. Every kiss, every touch—some people say the people they love energize them. When it comes to me and you, it's more literal. I literally am more powerful when I have you around, and all without taking anything from you."

"So with me here, you can... what can you do?"

He chuckles, dropping the cloth he's using to clean himself on the edge of the tub. "It's not endless, Heath. I can't do miracles. You're powerful, but not that powerful."

I keep staring at him, waiting for more of an answer, and he sighs. "I can fill a tub. If you call my name, I can come without it seemingly costing me any energy. As for the rest, I'm sure we'll find out together."

I like the sound of that. Together. Because we have time to figure it out, together.

We have a lifetime.

CHAPTER TWENTY-TWO

CHASE

We've only been asleep for a few hours when Heath's too-tight squeeze wakes me.

It's bordering on painful, and I'm genuinely worried he might crack one of my ribs as I try to worm out of his hold. "Heath?" I try, prying his arm open so I can slip out even as he resists my attempts. "Heath? Can you wake up?"

He whimpers, still squeezing me, so I close my eyes and visualize myself sitting on the far edge of the bed.

The magic leaves me light-headed, but I'm out of his hold now. His squeezing arms find nothing but air, and he shouts, waking up and moving upright, clearly ready to fight.

"It's me, Heath," I tell him, watching him carefully. His hands have tightened into fists, and his eyes are a little wild. "I'm here. We're safe."

His eyes snap to mine, and I watch him take several deep breaths as he stares at me intently. "Not the cages," he rasps.

"Not the cages," I agree.

"I dreamed…" He trails off, not ready to explain, although I think I can guess. He dreamed we were separated by the cages again. No wonder he'd squeezed me so tight. "Did I hurt you?"

"Just squeezed too tight. I'm fine."

He leans forward, trailing gentle fingers across my bare ribs, and I fight not to wince when he finds the sensitive part. It'll be healed soon enough.

He must see it on my face anyway, or else my scent changes in a way only a wolf would ever catch. "I'm so sorry."

"Don't be. I'm fine," I repeat, taking his hand and bringing it up to my mouth, kissing his fingertips. "How are you feeling?"

He opens his mouth like he wants to also say he's fine, but stops himself. He just watches me kissing his hand for a moment longer, then sighs. "That's actually helping."

I hum, pressing one kiss to the palm of his hand before bringing his hand down so I can look at him easier. I stroke my fingers along the veins of his wrist, keeping the touch slow and hopefully soothing. "I'm glad it helps. Tell me more."

Tell me everything, I want to say, but don't. He's barely able to admit that physical touch reassures him; I'm not going to get everything out of him tonight.

He's silent for a long moment. "I've never felt the wolf so close to the surface," he admits. "It's never supposed to be like that, and I turned twice in the cages and am worried I'm one scare from doing it again."

"Does it hurt you?"

"I'm not in control." He deflects from answering if it hurts. Or maybe that's answer enough for him. I'm guessing that being out of control of his own body would be akin to pain for someone like Heath.

I don't know how I'd feel about having a literal animal that could take over my body. I'd probably also not relish the thought. What I do know is that the wolf has tried to protect us both. That, when it was threatened, it tried to comfort me first and foremost. "What staves it off?"

He turns our hands so he's clasping mine, squeezing lightly. "You. If I know you're safe, then the wolf can settle. As long as you're safe, it's all fine."

"I'm safe, Heath." I don't mention the war brewing outside our door. We can leave that as a problem for later.

"Hence why I was squeezing you like that." He winces. "Sorry."

"Don't be sorry." I think about it for a moment. "I have an idea. If you're ready to try to go back to sleep?"

He looks skeptical but doesn't argue, just nods slightly, so I slowly withdraw my hand from his. "Lie down. On your side."

He does, and I waste no time lying down behind him and wrapping him in my arms. I make sure to squeeze lightly, pressing myself to him until I'm practically molded into the dip and curve of his spine. "There. You can't forget I'm here now." And he can't do any more than squeeze my arm. "Does this work?"

He fidgets for a minute, squirming to get comfortable. Then he takes one of my hands and brings it up so he can kiss it softly before returning it so I can securely re-fasten it around his middle. "It works. Thank you."

I kiss the back of his neck. "Anything for you."

It takes a long time for either of us to get back to sleep that night, but we eventually do, and I'll consider it a win.

Chapter Twenty-Three

Heath

When we were younger and trotted out for boring council meetings, Bryce and I would engage in staring contests to pass the time. Celia, the heir apparent, never got that luxury, but the two of us were quite competitive. It was perfect, because it was silent, required no materials, and was relatively deniable when we were caught.

At the ripe age of six hundred, I'd assumed that pastime was long behind me. And yet I've been engaged in a staring contest for several minutes, and I'm not even sure that the queen knows what she's doing.

Those blue eyes are peering into my very soul, unblinking, and she hasn't said a word all morning.

Chase isn't even here to reassure me that she'll get better. He woke up abruptly this morning muttering about being called, dressed quickly, and left.

So really, staring at the queen is preferable to worrying about him being out in Demonheim unprotected with the secrets he's keeping.

The doorknob turns, and I break the stare and am on my feet before I take a breath.

But then the door opens, and I can smell Chase, so I relax.

While I relax, the queen breaks her stare and practically runs away to her room, slamming the door behind her.

Chase, holding several plates of food stacked together in one hand, stares after her. "She say anything?"

Like she ever says anything in particular. I snort. "She's done nothing but stare at me with those creepy eyes for hours," I tell him, sparing half a glance to make sure her door is closed before talking about her this way. I don't know if I'd necessarily stop myself if she could hear, but I'd like to at least know.

I have sympathy for her, I really do. The cages continue to haunt my dreams—and, if I'm truly honest, they're never that far away during my waking hours, either—and the fact that she spent years in there is not lost on me. She deserves our sympathy and our help, and I would never deny her either.

I do wish she was more capable of being a help to us. Perhaps it's selfish, but it's true.

"Why do her eyes do that, anyways?" I ask, moving to help him with the plates. He doesn't really need help, of course, but I'll take any excuse to touch him after he's been out of the room. "I thought it might be a power thing, that she was so overloaded with power from being the queen, but her son's eyes don't do that."

"She's half furie," Chase says, setting the plates aside so he can trail one hand up my arm.

"Seriously?" That sends a shiver down my spine. "I thought they'd died out."

"Far as I know, her mother was the last. And she's definitely more demon than furie, but those eyes, they stick with you, right? Make you think she's seeing more than just what's on the surface."

That's exactly it. Those eyes are too unsettling for words. "Make you think she'll actually shoot lightning from her eyes."

"I'm pretty sure she can. I've never seen her do it, though."

And may we never see it. Especially not when she doesn't know who we are half the time.

But all that's irrelevant to the fact that Chase has been gone all day. "How did things go today?" I'm assuming since he's been chatting about the queen's history that no one has discovered his deception, but that doesn't mean everything is okay.

He sighs, rolling his neck and picking up one of the plates of food, walking it over to the queen's door and knocking lightly before setting it on the floor. We both now know from experience that she'll pick it up whenever she gets hungry enough.

"Things are unhinged. The king is sending demons out every day to make the worst kinds of deals with humans. He needs the power in this realm badly. But honestly right now, my biggest concern is that the demons who want out will do something foolish. It's obvious that there's no more secret portal out, but that doesn't mean they'll wait. I've tried subtly letting on to a few trusted people that there's a plan in the works, but I don't know if that will get around fast enough."

My muscles lock with tension. "That could be incredibly dangerous to you."

He snorts. "We're at war, Heath. I'm harboring the demon queen. I've been in contact with rebels and ferrying refugees for years now. I crossed into danger a long time ago. I've accepted it."

Maybe, but have I? Can I?

"Get over it, Heath," he says, crossing back over to me. "I am who I am. And who I am is someone in this up to my neck. Just like you." He sits on the sofa, using one hand to tug me down after him. He lets his head roll against the back of the sofa, closing his eyes. "Fate wouldn't pair us otherwise."

I wouldn't dare to even begin to guess at why fate pairs some people, and I also wouldn't dare to ever question why fate gave me Chase. If I did, I might upset the universe into taking him from me, and I simply wouldn't survive that.

Chase slings both his legs across my lap, sitting sideways on the sofa and pinning me in place, and all thoughts about anything besides him disappear.

I bask in the moment, in him holding me where he wants me, in him being here, for an untold amount of time before my stomach rumbles. I move to stand, but Chase just tightens his legs to pin me in place. "I need food, Chase."

Without even opening his eyes, he holds out one hand, and the plate disappears from the table and reappears in his hand. I blink at it. "Demon magic. Right."

His eyes are still closed, but he's smirking. "Comes in handy."

I take the food, and he opens his eyes enough so we can share the plate. "When you do your magic when we're together, it doesn't hurt you?" I check.

"I can't do the impossible," he clarifies. "I still have limits. It's like..." He thinks for a long minute. "I'm a bucket and my energy is the water inside. Every time I do magic, I poke a hole in the bucket. My energy might drain fast or slow, depending on the size of the hole. When I have you, you keep dumping more water in. So as long as you can dump it in faster than the water can drain out..."

That's actually the most sensible way he's described it yet, and I nod, picturing it in my head. Alright, I can work with that. "So, show me some more. Something that won't hurt you, please."

He watches me lazily for a minute, then nods. Little lights bounce around the room, bright glowing orbs floating around with no rhyme or reason.

"What is that?" I ask, watching one particularly bright one inches away from his head.

"An optical illusion. They're not real. Touch it."

I try, and my hand passes right through. It doesn't even feel like smoke, just entirely intangible, and I realize belatedly they carry no particular scent, either.

They all disappear in a shimmer, then are gone like they were never there in the first place.

I watch the space where one disappeared from. "But what's the point of that?" I ask.

A trickle of ice-cold water runs down the back of my shirt. When I turn to him, Chase looks entirely too innocent. "Magic doesn't have to have a point," he says. "We're demons. We like testing what we can do. Sometimes doing it is the whole point."

I consider that for a moment, then nod. The ways of demons don't have to entirely make sense to me, I suppose. And regardless, something warm blooms inside me when I watch him doing magic.

Even if it's dumping water down my shirt.

"Show me something else," I ask, taking his legs in my hand to pull him even more securely into me, stroking my thumb over his ankle bone as he debates what to show me next.

Chapter Twenty-Four

Chase

I'd say it's been a long day, but every day is a long day now.

The start of my days is always nice. I wake up wrapped around Heath, and even if nightmares still frequently shake our bed at night, I'd never want to sleep anywhere else.

The days tend to end well, too. We'll eat together, hold each other, and usually end the night with a spectacular orgasm.

It's the middle of the day that gets to me. I still have to go out into Demonheim, doing my best not to raise any suspicion. I would hope it would be easy, considering I did it for years, but it's a hundred times harder now. The secrets I'm keeping are somehow so much bigger, and affect far more than just me. Every day is a fight not to fall apart and give everything away.

Fariq won't take his eyes off of me. I don't think he knows, but I know that it's too much to hope that he doesn't suspect at least something. I'm not that impressive, yet I've supposedly been the sole survivor of the attack at the portal and the one who captured Heath. I suppose it would be stranger if it hadn't drawn some attention.

Still, the king had kept Fariq back today, so I'd considered it safe enough to sneak to the room where I used to meet rebels looking to escape and leave coded messages for those who knew where to look. Demonheim protects our secrets, and I'm relieved but not surprised when I make it to the room safely.

There's nothing new, which is a relief. The very last thing we need is people acting foolishly and risking us all getting caught.

We're close, I can feel it. If Demonheim can just hold on a little bit longer—

I slip back out of the room before anyone can notice, and move back towards my rooms.

***

Heath is putting together a little meal of all the remaining food we have when I enter, and I go up behind him, sliding my arms around his waist and plastering myself to his back. He doesn't stop working, although he uses one hand to clasp mine for a brief second.

It's the domesticity that makes my heart beat a little faster. The quietness of the moment, the sudden rush of peace now that I have him in my arms.

"How were things today?" he asks me, setting aside a finished plate.

"Same old, same old. And here?"

He shrugs. "I haven't seen her in hours. Will you knock and see if she'll come out?"

With great reluctance, I let him go, but not before I press a kiss to the back of his neck.

To my surprise, the door opens as soon as I knock, and the queen steps out, crossing the room with even strides to take a plate before she sits on the armchair closest to the fire.

Heath and I exchange long looks before we take our own food and sit across from her, watching her more intently than would be polite. There's a lucidity about her that we haven't seen before, a sureness to her movements, and neither of us is willing to let it slip away.

"What do you need me to do?" she asks after a moment, her voice quiet but nevertheless firm.

I know without asking that my queen is back. Truly back now, and not just her physical body.

I have no doubt that there will be regressions. Moments or hours or days where the cages take over again. But here, and now, she is with us, eyes clear and voice firm, even if her hands shake.

Heath speaks first. "What exactly do you remember?"

"My mate is dead," she says, and even now her voice doesn't waver. "He has been dead for some time. I don't know exactly how long; that part isn't clear yet. But he's dead. His brother…" She takes a deep, shaky breath. "Where is my son?"

Her son. She hasn't mentioned Ryder yet, not once in all the time she's been free of the cages. She likely forgot him in an attempt to shut out memories of his father. But here she is, asking after him. She remembers.

"He's not here," Heath says.

"Obviously. Where is he?"

She sounds so queenly, so regal when she says it. I remember when she was my queen. I didn't know her well—there was nothing special about me, after all—but this firmness, this no-nonsense attitude, is exactly what I expect from a queen.

"He's leading a camp of rebels," I tell her. "Refugees, mostly. Demons running from Demonheim. Him and his mate are planning a coup."

She goes very still for a second, like she's searching her memory. "Hannah?" She asks, like she needs to confirm who her son mated.

"Yes, Hannah."

She nods, seemingly satisfied. "Always liked her."

From what I've heard, that's a lie. Not that the queen ever did anything especially bad to her, but Hannah's existence as a halfling, never being demon enough, had certainly been less than pleasant.

I don't mention it to the queen. It wouldn't be productive.

Besides, if Hannah still has grievances, she's more than capable of handling them herself, and her husband will certainly support her. She doesn't need me fighting her battles for her.

"And where do you come into this?" she asks, eyeing me so sharply that she must know who I am.

It's not like my father ever introduced us. He didn't bring me around when he was married to her. I didn't attend family functions. I wasn't there to act as Ryder's older brother.

But she knows who I am, I'm certain of it.

Heath clears his throat before I have to think up an answer. "Hannah is a friend of mine. We actually, we were the ones who dug up that sword. So, she asked me for my help to dethrone him now."

I start, looking away from the queen and to my mate. "You found it?" I demand, shock twisting my insides.

He flashes me a pained smile. "What, you thought I was just a pretty face, Chase? I'll have you know Hannah and I served on a lot of fronts together. With a knack at being in the right place at the right time. Whether that's for spying, for battle, or just recovering lost relics. Of course, digging up that one... well, I regret it." He pauses for a second. "Mostly. But it brought me to you, so I can't lie. I'm still partially grateful."

What a wolfish thing to say, I think for a moment. Everyone knows wolves would endure anything, any pain, any loss, for their mates.

Then again, can I really say I feel any different?

"I would have found you regardless," I tell him, because that must be true. We can't live in a world where it isn't true.

He smiles at me, something so soft and heartbreakingly sweet, and it takes all my willpower to turn back to the queen. "Your son doesn't know you're alive yet. I haven't been able to get word to him."

I would have loved to send him a note, even if *your mother is alive and suffering from prolonged confinement in the cages* seems like an unfair thing to say over a military brief. But without access to the portal, I don't have a way to send him word.

"And going to him isn't an option?" She looks at me shrewdly, calculating her options.

If she's rational enough to access her own magic, she might be able to tell the realm to open a portal for her. She's the queen, after all. The realm will respond to her in ways it never would to me. Still, I hesitate. "We were thinking that the three of us might be more useful here."

She raises an eyebrow. "That's a lot of faith to put in a broken old queen."

It's a challenge, a gauntlet thrown down between us. Heath rises to the occasion admirably.

"I'm a wolf," he says simply. "We know to never underestimate a queen."

An understatement. I've heard about his sister.

Queen Olette smiles at him, something sharp and biting. Demonic, one might say.

"What can I do?"

Chapter Twenty-Five

Chase

So, we begin to plan.

Between the three of us, conversations can become relatively chaotic, with three people with strong opinions all in the same room. It's especially bad because Heath and the queen are both used to having their opinions listened to, and neither is great at backing down.

I wonder if it's Heath's royal blood that lets him argue with a queen without flinching, or if his sister actually allows this type of dissent towards her.

Even with all our arguing and planning, the plan remains relatively simple. I'm going to stop pretending to serve the king and instead rally whoever I can into open rebellion, both to serve as a distraction and to clear the way for Ryder. Heath will use his skills at being places where I shouldn't, as he calls it, to both steal the sword and get the queen on the throne. At that point, she will take power over the realm and immediately open the way to Ryder and Hannah. From there, Heath will hand the sword to Ryder and Ryder will finish our father.

Arguing over that had taken time. Heath hates the idea of me being the one to lead a rebellion, citing it as too dangerous. When I point out that stealing the sword and throne is equally dangerous, he attempts to brush it off.

I don't let him, though.

"You're my mate, too," I tell him softly. We're in bed. Heath had fucked me deep and almost aggressive. I think part of it might be frustration with my stubbornness, but it's probably also desperation. To hold me, to have me. To confirm I'm here when we discuss dangerous things.

I don't blame him. I feel it too, this desperate need to hold him, have him. To know he's mine and not going anywhere.

At least, not yet.

"And as my mate, I worry about you," I continue. I flick his nose gently, making him scrunch it up adorably. "Don't think you have a monopoly on that, Heath."

He stares at me for a long minute, but at long last nods. "I'm sorry," he says.

His voice is still low, rough, the type of tone he has when he's whispering sweet, filthy promises in my ear. I shiver.

"Listen to me," I say, and I roll so I'm straddling him. He hardens under me, his cock pressing against my ass, and I can't resist rocking my hips just slightly. "We have a long future ahead of us, right?"

He stares at me, mouth hanging open in rapture. "Yes."

"So trust me: I'm not going to die on you before I get that." I rock my hips again, just to see his face. "I want that future, Heath. I want it with everything I have. So we're both going to walk away from this." I rock again, and his hands come up to my hips, impatient now, ready to guide me where he needs me. I let him, just as desperate to go again.

"Besides," I say, panting a bit as he slides into my still-slick hole, "I might not have the strength of a wolf, but you haven't seen me in a fight yet. I can hold my own."

He doesn't say anything else. Whether I convinced him or he's just focused on how it feels to be inside me, I can't say, but I take full advantage of the end of the conversation.

There are better things to do than talk.

***

Only the next day, Heath hasn't dropped it. "What would I do to give you the energy to summon a sword?" he asks.

I raise an eyebrow. "You'd look under the bed. But I wouldn't say no to anything else you want to do. Energy or no."

Unfortunately for me, he scrambles out of bed, going to his hands and knees to look under my bed. I admire the flex of his muscles, his ass essentially stuck straight up in the air.

Just when I start wondering if that counts as an invitation, he stands, pulling out two of the swords I've hidden beneath the bed. He studies them, unimpressed. "These aren't even properly sharp."

That seems a bit of an over-exaggeration, because they could definitely still cut a man.

"There's a whetstone under there too," I tell him, half in defense and half to see if he'll bend over again to get it. Sadly, he just continues to stare at my swords, not even acknowledging what I just told him.

"No," he says after a moment. "Dull might be better for our purpose."

I blink at him. "And what purpose could that possibly be?"

"You're going to show me what you got." he tells me, voice entirely serious.

"This doesn't seem necessary—" I start to say, but his looks silences me.

He just extends one of the swords to me, not saying anything while waiting for me to take it.

"You're serious."

"Absolutely."

"Where do you plan to do this?" I challenge, taking the sword from him and looking it over.

He just raises an eyebrow. "Your sitting room. It's not much bigger than the average corridor you plan to fight in."

He has a point, so I sigh and get out of bed. "Am I allowed to put pants on first?"

"The queen might not like it if you forget. And while I'm sure it would heal, there's parts of you I'd prefer not to do damage to," he teases, breaking into a small smile.

So I find myself facing off against my mate, swords drawn, in my sitting room while the queen watches us. The worst part is Heath doesn't seem even marginally winded by my strikes; indeed, he has enough breath to offer criticism as we go.

"I'm not a bad swordsman, you know," I protest after the better part of an hour, trying to strike at his seemingly exposed shoulder. He blocks instantly.

"No, you're not," he allows, immediately undercutting it by sneaking an attack under my guard. "But you're not great, either. You could use training."

"How much time do you think we have, Heath?" I ask as I strike back, which he side-steps neatly.

"As much time as it takes to keep you safe. Everything else can wait."

He's a mated wolf, I remind myself. He's a mated wolf who, very recently, was in enough danger that his wolf side was brought to the surface. Surely that explains him being willing to let the realm suffer so he can train me to whatever standard he thinks is appropriate.

"I might not fight like a wolf," I agree, blocking his next attack, "But I know how to fight like a demon."

And then I suck the light out of the room.

Heath is a wolf and can likely see quite well in the dark, but I'm mostly after the complete, split-second disorientation of the world changing unexpectedly.

No one ever expects demon magic.

Like I suspected would happen, Heath's momentarily off balance, and I use that moment to strike, bringing my dull sword blade close enough to his neck to make my point.

I preserve the darkness for a long moment, then let the light return to the room. The candles continue to flicker like nothing has changed. For them, nothing has; I never extinguished them. The darkness simply covered them entirely.

Heath blinks at me, then smiles. The smile is a slow unfolding, like it's just occurring to him what exactly he witnessed.

"I'm convinced," he says. "Can you do that without overexerting yourself?"

The queen huffs. "With you around? He'll be fine."

We both turn to her. To tell the truth, I'd almost forgotten she was there.

"Can you fight, your majesty?" Heath asks.

"If you get me to that throne, this realm will respond to my every whim. It will yield entirely to me. I won't need to fight; the realm will do it for me."

"I'll take that as a no, then," Heath says dryly. He pauses to consider, but seemingly decides that handing her a blade might not be our best choice. "I'll keep that in mind."

Heath turns away from her, setting his sword carefully aside before turning to me. "I think you deserve some sort of reward. Victor's spoils," he says, eyes bright and wicked.

Chapter Twenty-Six

Heath

C hase plays dirty, and that somehow makes me desperate to fuck.

I suppose I shouldn't be shocked. I know plenty of wolves who get turned on by a tumble on the training field and find bed partners that way; I've done it myself, a time or two.

But nothing in all my years has ever made me quite as desperate as that clever, calculating glint in Chase's eyes.

Gods, I can't decide if I want to wipe that look off his face, or stare up and see that look in his eyes as he makes me fall apart.

Just when I'm debating if I can somehow make both happen, Chase grabs my arm and starts dragging me towards the bedroom. "Victor's spoils," he repeats, closing the door behind us.

Well. The queen is more alert now, at least. If she doesn't want to hear us, she seems rational enough to go into her room on the other side of the sitting area.

"How do you want this?" I ask, because I suppose as the victor it's his right to choose.

"I want... I want..." he trails off, like he's having the same problem I am—too many options to choose from.

I can help him with that. I step closer, right into his face, bringing my mouth close to his ear. "I could suck you," I whisper. "Your choice if you want my mouth on your cock or your horns."

"Gods, Heath, you are—" he doesn't finish the thought, so I never find out exactly what he thinks I am. Instead, he kisses me until I start to feel light-headed, biting kisses that leave me aching for more as he guides me backwards, pushing me towards the bed.

"I'm going to ride your cock," he tells me, that calculating glint back in his eyes, and it's all I can do to nod rapidly. Fuck, yes. Whatever he wants. "What you do with my horns while I ride your cock is your business."

I tug at my own trousers, raising my hips to remove them so I can sit on the bed, watching Chase get his clothes off so he can ride me like he wants.

I'm going to make him see fucking stars.

Once his trousers are gone, Chase closes his eyes for a moment to make the vial of oil appear in his hand. I watch him for a moment, trying to determine if this magic so quickly on the heels of what he did during our sword fight would hurt him, but he doesn't react at all.

Well, that's one thing off my mind, at least. He'll be able to use his magic to fight during the upcoming coup, and he won't pass out—or kill himself—if he needs more than one act of magic.

But I don't want to think about what's coming. That is a problem for tomorrow. Right now, the only problem is how to make my mate come.

"Sit on my lap," I invite, patting my thighs as if he needs a visual re-minder.

He straddles my legs, settling in with rather more rocking and rubbing than I'd think necessary. I smile, then kiss his neck, teasing at the pulse point that makes his groan.

"Kneel up," I whisper against his skin. "And open yourself for me while I make you feel good."

"You're pushy for someone who didn't actually win," he says, but his voice is already slightly breathless.

I bite at his neck. "We can have a re-match, if you'd rather?"

I hear the vial being uncorked, apparently the only response I'm going to get. It sends a clear enough message, regardless.

I lick over the spot on his neck I just bit, soothing the wound, before I start to worry at the spot with my lips and teeth. Chase likes being bitten, I've learned, which makes him the perfect mate for a wolf, considering how much we like to bite.

Then, when he's ready to begin fingering himself, I reach up and fondle his horns. He gasps, mouth hanging open as I stroke one sensual finger over the left horn, while leaning up to trail my tongue over the right.

He shudders over me so violently that I place my free hand on his hip, holding him steady. And then I suck the very tip of his horn into my mouth.

The point is slightly sharp, so I'm careful not to stab my tongue as I lick around it, finding every sensitive spot.

"Do you want me to come before you're even inside me?" Chase asks, voice strained.

"I think I'm skilled enough to get you there twice," I say back, breathing against his horn as I do, making him shudder again. "So do what you need to."

He grunts, then I feel one of his hands, slick with oil, on my cock, and the other on my shoulder. "Now," he says. "I want you in me now, Heath, come on—"

He's pleading for something he can give himself, but I back off of teasing him for a moment, in case that's what he's asking for.

It seems to be, because he grabs my cock to steady it and sinks down onto me. And then I'm inside him, and the entire world re-aligns until we are the only two beings in existence, until he is all I can feel, all I can see, all I can smell.

Fuck. My entire brain turns to mush, thinking only by the way his mouth is slightly open, his eyes half closed, his hips jerking slightly as he gets used to me inside him again.

I'm worried I'm going to come immediately. He's so tight and hot, a vise around my cock, and so fucking beautiful above me.

And then he starts to move.

"Fuck, Chase—" I groan, hands gripping his hips, breath panting against his skin as I try to bring us that much closer, like the few inches between us are an intolerable gap. His cock rubs against my stomach, leaving a sticky mess of precome, and I squeeze his hips at the feel of it. "You are so perfect. So damned perfect."

One of his hands finds my hair, running through it and then tugging when he gets to the roots. I groan, my head falling back, my eyes finding his immediately. "You feel so damned good," he tells me, and I can't resist him.

Wolves are particularly averse to the idea of having a type, because we don't know who our mates will eventually be. So I've never considered a particular set of characteristics more beautiful than another before, but how could I ever not have?

How did I not know clever dark eyes, sandy hair, and black horns would be my undoing?

"You're so fucking beautiful," I tell him, unable to resist rocking my hips, trying to thrust up to meet him.

He is beautiful, truly beautiful, but I know he's going to be even more beautiful when he comes, so I return to teasing his horns with one hand, and use the other to stroke his cock.

"Oh fuuuckk," he groans, low and deep, more vibration than sound, as he comes around me, squeezing me so deliciously, perfectly tight.

And I can't help but follow him down.

"Fuck, that was good. I need to beat you in fights more often," Chase says, letting his whole body weight sag against me after.

I chuckle darkly and flip us so he's on his back, sprawled on the blankets. I crawl over him, and his eyes go dark once more. Lust, yes, but also that clever, conniving look.

Well, this is a struggle I plan to win. "I'm not done with you," I tell him.

Not in the slightest. My mate, fucked out and warm and smelling so delicious—that requires exploring.

Chapter Twenty-Seven

Chase

After our sword practice—and the ensuing hours of sex—Heath has to admit that we're as ready as we're ever going to be. Short of getting word to Ryder, there's nothing else we can do.

The last obstacle is ensuring that the queen is ready.

She seems more rational each and every day. She's able to engage in conversation with us, recalling details of Demonheim and seeming to grasp what we're discussing. There are still times where her attention wanders, but I suppose that can't be helped.

So we move forward. I put out word that I'm looking for sympathetic demons, and while I won't know if there is a response until the moment is right, I have hope. We go over the plan a thousand more times, discussing every possible scenario.

The last thing Heath does is sharpen my admittedly neglected swords. He keeps shooting me worried looks, but he's not saying anything.

I'm choosing to read it as a general worry, and not doubt in our ability to do this.

I have to believe we can do this. For my home, for my king, for all of us—this needs to work.

I lean over and kiss the top of his head. "Anything else that needs doing?"

Heath sighs, setting the whetstone aside and handing me a sword. "Just a waiting game now," he says.

So we wait.

***

Once the evening creeps in, we get up without a word, strapping on swords and moving towards the door. "Stay behind me," Heath tells the queen, and then we're silent.

I haven't been able to confirm that anyone got the message I left in the secret room. I'd barely been able to dodge watching eyes long enough to leave the message and haven't been back since.

It doesn't need to be many demons. Just enough to seem serious, to seem like a danger. Just enough to draw my father's attention away from his throne and what Heath does.

Too soon, I feel Heath and the queen fade away into the shadows behind me. They don't say anything—silence is the point, after all—but I know the moment they're gone.

Two corridors later, and I'm in front of the door. Taking a deep breath, I push it open.

There's a small crowd waiting on the other side and seeing how many people saw my call is a sharp, instant relief.

"We haven't seen you in a while," Fargus says, eyeing me across the table, his knife clenched tight in his hand.

"I've been busy," I tell him. "But I'm here now. And I need your help."

"You find another way out?" he demands.

Fargus has wanted out of Demonheim for a while now, and no doubt feels the sting of the portal being compromised more than just about anyone. "No," I tell him. "But we're going to take Demonheim. If you'll follow me."

He raises an eyebrow. "No one can take Demonheim. You've seen that sword?"

"Course he's seen that sword," someone else says. "Chase is always right next to the king, isn't he?"

That hurts, but I don't acknowledge it. "What if I told you the queen was alive?"

"I'd say you're full of shit."

I take a deep breath. "She's alive," I tell them. "And she's ready to claim her throne. All she needs is enough people to distract the king until she gets it done."

"Sounds like you're trying to get people to turn traitor—how do we know it's not a set up?"

"I'm here, aren't I?" I ask, impatience clipping my words. "I think just being here is probably enough to count as treason."

"Which would be an ideal way to set us up," someone says. "Turn us in and spare yourself."

"I think I'm already in this too deep for that," I protest.

It takes half an hour to convince them that I'm not just setting them up to die. But eventually, I get nearly twenty of them to agree to follow me. I look around, seeing the determined faces, and don't know what to say. We could all die together today. Heath is the only thing between us and that possibility.

But he's my mate, and I trust him.

"Let's go, then," I say, and head to the exit.

And as soon as I open the door, I'm faced with two dozen soldiers, with my father at their front.

"Well, well," he says, smirk clear on his face. "I'm disappointed, Chase."

Chapter Twenty-Eight

Chase

I gape at him, having no idea what to say, having no idea how to defend all the people behind me.

"How did you know?" I ask, voice quiet, hoping to disguise the trembling.

This is still salvageable, a part of my brain reminds me. My father has the sword, as always, so we are in dire danger here. But if we can get the queen on the throne, then there is a chance for the future of Demonheim.

Whether or not any of us here will live to see that chance is unclear.

"Plenty of people have been suspicious of you," the king says, looking at me down his nose, disgust turning the corners of his mouth.

It's shame for his embarrassment of a son, and a part of me remembers how, years and years ago, I wanted him to like me. I wanted to mean something to him. To anyone, really.

But that all changed. I'll die before I make him happy.

"I tried," he says, "to give you the background to go with your breeding. I try to do everything in my power to utilize the blood that ran through your veins. You disappoint me, Chase."

Being near death apparently makes me bold. "You've long since disappointed me," I tell him. "I suppose that makes us even."

His lip curls. "Big talk for a man about to die."

There is no sense in pretending that this isn't what it looks like. I am here to distract him with a rebellion, after all, and it doesn't matter if we didn't get to choose the time and place. I draw my sword, holding it up, ready for my last stand.

"Run," I say to those behind me, and a split second later, I suck all the light out of the hallway.

I hear clattering footsteps, but also swords being drawn. My opponents? Or those behind me choosing to stand and fight?

And then light returns to the space, and the king is inches from my face, that terrifying sword raised. "You think this realm gives you more than it does me?" he asks, voice thunderous. "You think you're worth anything? You think you're special? Anything you can do, I can do."

But I have a mate. I'm not stupid enough to shout it out like I want to—that's the last thing he needs to know right now. Still, it's true. Having a mate gives me an edge. Even with the little bit of extra magic Demonheim gives him for being the false king, I could still beat him. My energy from my mate will outlast him.

It's that sword that tips the balance towards him, and I can't take my eyes off it.

Why hasn't he done it? If he's written me off, if he's seen what I've done...

He leans closer, and I think that this is it. This is the last moment I'll live, and I take a second to regret that I'll never see Heath again. That we're over before we started, really. That a few stolen moments in my bed are all we'll ever have, that our dreams of a future are already lost.

But then the king just holds his sword to my throat. "You think I don't know about your foolish little plans?" he hisses to me, like this is a private conversation that must be kept from the soldiers around us. "You're a fool with an inflated sense of your own skills if you think you slipped past me and mine, Chase. We've been watching you. We've been waiting for you to step out of line. And we've easily guessed who you're hiding in those rooms of yours."

He grabs my arm with the hand not holding a sword to my throat. "Your little rebellion better scramble, or my men will cut them down," he says. "But you won't be here to see it."

And then he makes us both disappear.

Chapter Twenty-Nine

Heath

Walking away from my mate hurts.

I can remind myself of that plan a thousand times, saying it over and over in my head. I can remind myself that Chase has power, that he can look after himself. I can remind myself that this is the promise I made Hannah, that I said I would defend this realm.

I can remind myself of those things every second we walk away, but it doesn't change the fact that I'm walking away from my mate, and that the wolf inside me violently rejects doing so.

"Faster," I murmur, eyeing the queen as I drag her along behind me. I'm much more casual regarding royalty than others might be—it would be difficult not to be, after spending so many years wrestling and arguing with the queen of the werewolves—but even I know that dragging a queen by the arm is poor manners.

I'll owe her an apology later. For now, I have a task to complete.

"Just up ahead," she murmurs, just before the throne room emerges into view.

"C'mon," I urge, tugging on her arm rudely once more.

But she doesn't move, like her legs are planted into the ground. "Something is wrong," she murmurs, one hand trailing over the air, like she's stroking something invisible.

"What's wrong?" I ask with as much patience as I can.

Those electric-lightning blue eyes flash at me, sheer determination in her eyes. This isn't madness, or uncertainty, and her sureness makes me freeze. "You think I don't know when something is wrong in my own realm?" she challenges me, her fingers still rapidly moving. It looks like she's plucking at something, pulling invisible strings as she speaks. "You think this realm that birthed me, nurtured me—that I gave my life force for, that I am queen of—you think I don't know when something is wrong here?" Her hands stutter for a short second. "He's coming."

And that's all the warning we get before the king appears, his sword at Chase's throat, eyes promising merciless death.

I drop the queen's wrist. That sword, that sword that promises swift death, even to beings like us... and it's so close to his throat...

I fight to keep the wolf from forcing its way out of me. It won't do any good here, as desperately as it wants to defend its mate.

"Let's talk," I say, trying to project confidence in my voice. Trying to sound like I have things under control, like there is even a scrap of rationality left inside me.

His smile is cold, and merciless, and cruel. "Let's," he agrees. "We have a lot to talk about, don't we, spy?"

Footsteps pound down the corridor, and a dozen guards fall in, standing directly behind their king.

I swallow. "What do you want?"

"You know what I want. But I'm not here to negotiate, wolf. It seems to me that I hold all the bargaining power; you need to listen to what I say."

"I'm listening," I say carefully.

He's not going to offer us any reasonable terms. His insistence that he holds all the power tells me he plans for this to end one way: with our blood soaking into the gaudy, magma-red lines on his marble flooring.

But I need to keep him talking. Every moment he's focused on me is one he isn't focused on Chase, and one more moment I have to find a way out of this for us.

"You have something that belongs to me," he says.

I can't think of what he possibly means until it dawns on me. "Your wife?" I demand incredulously, unaware this man could possibly make me even sicker than I already am.

"She's mine," he repeats. "And I'll have her back."

"So you can torture her again?"

"I never laid a finger on her."

"You never spent any time in the cages, have you?" I ask rhetorically, mind spinning to try to keep up.

He needs her back. He needs to shove her back in the cages, weakening her power over the realm and strengthening his own.

And then he can kill Chase and I, and Ryder's plan will be hobbled for a while longer.

He's right; he holds a lot of the power. But not all of it.

"Chase!" I shout, pouring as much intention behind the word as I can, hoping he'll know. Hoping the magic knows, that this most basic demon contract will know when it's being called on.

It was the mention of the cages that did it, knowing how Chase helped me escape. Remembering what he told me about demon bargains, and how the magic works. Hoping against hope that calling his name will work once more.

With grateful eyes, he starts to disappear right out of the king's hold.

"Run," I tell the queen, now that I can take action without immediately losing my mate.

Chase appears at my side as the queen turns to run. I brace, ready to push back the king until she reaches her throne, and I see Chase adjusting his stance next to me, ready to fight at my side.

Except she doesn't run towards the throne. She turns and bolts, running out of the throne room. Her eyes flash, and the soldiers that stand in her way fall down, smoking, burning holes carved into their torsos. Then, she's entirely out of sight.

"No!" I shout, but I cut myself off. She left. There's nothing I can do about that, nothing I can do to make her stay.

Chase and I still need to stand and fight. If we can just get that sword...

I risk a look at Chase. He holds his sword at the ready, his face set in a line of grim determination. He, too, already knows our odds without either of us having to say anything.

"Ask me to take you away from here," he murmurs, just loud enough for the two of us to hear him, keeping the words from the king and his guards. "Ask me."

I don't ask. He doesn't ask me again, either. We both know it is not an option either of us will take.

He nods once, defeat already evident across his face. I see him open his mouth and then close it again.

I don't know what to say either.

How does one say goodbye to a mate they had for such a short time? It seems cruel for fate to pair us up and then to tear us apart so quickly.

Cruel, but I wouldn't have it any other way. If I was always destined to die today, I'm grateful for every second I got with Chase first.

I turn away from Chase. I have to; if I keep looking at him, I won't be able to do what needs to be done.

So I charge. No sense waiting around for the end to come; wolves always like the offensive more, anyway.

I can feel Chase at my back without turning to look. The wolf tracks the movements of every member of the pack instinctually, always knowing exactly where they are in any fight.

I keep my attention forward, parrying the king's swing. Perhaps he's actually a weak swordsman, letting his murderous blade pick up the slack. If that's true, then I can outmatch him. I just have to avoid any potentially lethal strikes.

If I can take him out at the wrist, then I can end this. His hand would eventually regenerate, but it would do the job for now, taking his sword and preventing him from fighting today.

The plan solidifies in my mind, already thinking several steps ahead. I know strategy; I know how people fight, how they move. I know how to anticipate attacks, how to adjust. I know how to win.

And when he strikes back, moves backed with enough force to knock me back a step, I know instantly that all my planning is for nothing.

This man knows what he's doing. He has soldiers, and magic, and a sword that can make all my wounds mortal.

I am going to die.

CHAPTER THIRTY

CHASE

We're absolutely, irrevocably fucked.

The queen ran. I should have expected it and should have anticipated her losing control. It doesn't stop me from feeling the hot flush of anger, the realization that she left us here to die.

The most charitable parts of me can consider that she's hurt and scared. That maybe she'll live and be able to fight another day.

And that's all true. But it doesn't change that Heath and I will be dead.

I should have asked for a more thorough lesson about sword fighting, I think grimly, squaring off against one of my father's loyal guards. I can still use magic to aid me, but the sheer size of the force we're facing is certainly terrifying.

We're going to die here. I don't see a way around that. I suppose it doesn't matter if I can fight well or not.

The best I can hope for is to buy Heath a few extra moments. Maybe he can do something with the time. Maybe he can win.

He should have let me get him out of here. This shouldn't be his fight.

Then one of the guards knicks me with his sword. I bare my teeth and shove back, placing my sword through his gut. It won't kill him, but it will put him on the ground for a while, and that's all I need. No more thoughts of what could have been. There is only here, and now.

I step over him, and turn to the next demon to raise a sword to me.

I parry the next sword swung my way, then crack the floor beneath the guard's feet. Using that power so soon after teleporting to Heath makes my vision blur for just a second, but I can keep going.

I keep moving, wanting to get myself closer to Heath. I'm not sure if my goal is to help him or just to die at his side. Maybe it's both.

Thrust, parry, move. Over and over again, and my vision narrows, my entire focus just on the next move, the next step, the next bloody path.

And then there's a sword at my throat.

I curse, trying to duck out of the way of the man who has drawn up behind me with the blade. But I can't move without cutting my own head off.

"Chase!" Heath shouts, panic coating his voice, irrepressible. The collected, focused wolf is gone, replaced by this desperate, intense man in front of me.

His voice is laden with the promise of a demon contract, coated with that compelling need to go to his side. I close my eyes, and then I disappear straight out of danger, pulled towards him.

When I reappear at his side, when the world comes into focus again, a scream of pain pierces the air.

I turn towards him, already on the defensive, to see his hand over his face. Blood drips between his fingers, and my heart stops.

"Distracted, wolf?" My father taunts.

My stomach curdles. What did he do to Heath's face? How badly is he hurt?

Heath lowers his hand and I see the damage. Heart sinking, I take in his face, slashed through the eye with blood gushing from the wound.

Heath's face is twisted with pain, and through all the blood, I can't even tell if his eye is still in his head.

"That's the thing about mates," my father growls at him. "You become weaker just by their very existence."

Not true. Heath's existence has only made me stronger in so many ways, ways my father would never understand.

A man who manipulates his grieving sister-by-fate into marrying him, who locks her in the cages, who can be as cold to his son as my father is—that is a man who simply doesn't understand true bonds. And a man like that can't be convinced. I won't waste my breath arguing with him. Instead, I lunge forward, hoping to catch him off guard, hoping that I can get one clean strike.

He's prepared for me, one step ahead just like always. He pushes me back with one well-placed, seemingly effortless block.

I lunge again. I can't help it, and am nearly mindless with it now. There is no other option; if we're going to die here, if he's going to speak about my mate like that, then I'll take him down with me.

He sneers at me as he continues to bat away my attacks like they're nothing. "I always knew you'd be a disappointment," he muses, not even winded by our continued exchange of strikes. It's like I'm a particularly annoying fly that he's swatted away but hasn't squashed yet. "I suppose part of that blame lies with me; I never took the time to make you into anything worthwhile. I thought breeding would win the day, but, well, clearly it hasn't."

"Both your sons fight against you," I reply, forcing the words out even though I know I should ignore him and his taunts and focus on my attacks. "Both of us hate you. Maybe it is breeding after all. Maybe there's something about you."

He snarls and lunges forward in response. I manage to evade, but just barely, taking another step back, ceding even more ground. "And I would never want to be anything like you," I tell him.

"Insolent brat, I—"

A sword clashes down between us, disrupting whatever insult he planned to hurl at me next. Heath jumps between us, blood still dripping down his face. I wonder if he can even see anything, but his strikes are sure, his footwork confident.

"Something you should know about wolves," he says, striking fast enough to put my father back on the defensive. "Our sense of sight isn't nearly as important as our sense of smell."

Sure enough, he unerringly finds my father. Each strike is true, and he keeps moving, faster and faster.

With my heart in my throat, I break the awful marble floor, trying my best to time it perfectly so it will disrupt my father's steps and not Heath's, knowing that he won't be able to see the obstacle coming.

The floor cracks. The king stumbles, and Heath's strike drives true, slicing right through the tendons of his forearm.

Both the severed arm and the sword clatter to the floor, followed a split second later by the furious, shocked howling of my father.

I don't think, just act; I summon every last wisp of energy I have left while running closer, getting one hand on Heath and the other on my father's blood-stained sword. Then, I disappear, bringing the two of us to the other side of the throne room.

We have the sword. Heath really did turn this fight for us.

The victory is short-lived, however. Heath is still bleeding, and I'm starting to tip listlessly as we stand here. We're holding the sword, but I'm not confident either of us could swing it right that moment.

And then there's a clattering of feet in the hall.

Chapter Thirty-One

Heath

I can't see anything.

If I cover my left eye, I can perceive blurry shapes that seem oddly flat, which is next to useless to me. Luckily, I'm a wolf, and every other sense is exactly as important, and exactly as strong.

I smell the damage I did to the king. I can even smell Chase's exhaustion and desperation. I can smell that cursed blade he's holding, too. Death and blood and misery cling to every inch of the metal blade, and I would toss it away from us forever if it wasn't our only chance at survival.

And I can smell the crush of bodies in the hallway.

I recognize Hannah, then Ryder, and there—that's the queen, too. My heart beats faster.

She didn't abandon us. She brought reinforcements.

What a way for Ryder to find out that his mother is actually alive.

The gathering crowd of demons pours into the throne room, and steel clashes immediately, Hannah and Ryder's soldiers against the remaining guards.

I don't bother turning to look when Ryder steps alongside us. "We have something for you," I say, and Chase hands him the sword.

He doesn't say anything back, but I wouldn't expect him to. There's a place you have to go, when you're in the heat of battle like this, that doesn't leave much room for speaking. I'd imagine that's only exacerbated by what he needs to do.

His footsteps are sure and determined as he moves to kill his father.

I don't begrudge him the kill, talking the wolf inside me down from the vengeance it's demanding as I turn so I can catch my swaying mate in my arms.

"We did it," I murmur in his ear. "We make a pretty good team," I tell him, clinging tighter to him. I'm not sure which one of us I'm keeping upright, at this point.

He laughs shortly. "We do. But if it's all the same, I sincerely hope we never need to be this type of team again."

I hear when the blade severs the skin on the king's neck, then smell the blood spilling all over the gaudy floor. As soon as his head hits the ground with a decisive thump, the clash of steel stops.

The king is dead.

There's silence so deep that I can pick out the individual breaths of everyone in the room for a long, long moment. Then Ryder says, voice deep but even, "Mother, the throne is yours."

The silence continues, and I think a few of us are actually holding our breaths, waiting for her to say something.

I try to subtly scent the air, realizing I'm the only non-demon present. I am the only outsider witnessing this, this moment among the notoriously private and guarded demons.

Of course, I'm barely witnessing it. Scenting the beings in the room is all well and good—and has just handily saved my and Chase's life—but it makes for poor story-telling later.

The queen finally speaks. "No."

"Mother—"

"I said no, Ryder. I'm rational enough to know how that ends." She's silent for a minute, then says, "I know he's dead today. What if I don't tomorrow? If I have full control of this realm, if I think he's been ripped away from me—" The silence feels even heavier than before. "You're young, Ryder. With a strong mate. She'll support you. I'll support you where I can. The throne is yours."

I wonder how Hannah is feeling, being explicitly praised by the demon queen. She wanted demons to accept her for so long—and now the former queen is carving out her place at the almost-king's side.

Ryder takes a deep, heavy breath. I can smell the blood on him, although none of it smells like his own.

Hannah, on the other hand, has bled today. Not too badly, I think, but she has definitely bled. I recognize the tang of it, sharp in the air, and recognize what she was willing to sacrifice to get her mate here to this throne room.

She would have died for him, I know without asking. I know because I would have done the same for Chase today, in a heartbeat, a thousand times over.

"You do this with me," Ryder says to Hannah, and the words sound like an order but the tone like a plea.

"I will," she agrees, and then footsteps echo away from us and towards the throne.

I hear the footsteps stop, the rustle of clothes. Then the silence thickens, like everyone in this room is waiting for something.

When it happens, I don't feel it. But everyone around me does, judging by the sharp spike in the tension and the way Chase almost collapses in my hold.

Then again, that could just be his exhaustion.

I want to ask him what's happening. I want to ask him how to help him, if I should take him somewhere else. I want to ask him to check the damage done to my eye. But I keep silent, not wanting to be the first to speak.

"It's done," Ryder says, and I don't think it's my imagination that his voice sounds even deeper than before, an echo behind it that was not there when we spoke in his camp. "Tell my people—tell them to come home."

He's a young king. But Celia was a young queen. Celia had us three siblings supporting her and, when she finally allowed it, Bethany, too. Likewise, Ryder will have support.

I know Hannah, and she won't let him fail. Through blood, and sweat, and war if need be, she will ensure he succeeds.

Good, I think. Good, that it's all come together. Good, that this place will be taken care of, that there are people we can rely on here.

And, like knowing the job is done is the permission my body needs, the pain in my eye becomes so unbearable that I pass out.

CHAPTER THIRTY-TWO

CHASE

Heath's body goes slack against mine, sending me tumbling to the ground too. We both land in a heap on the throne room floor—already looking less like the human's approximation of hell and more like the soft white marble I remember from before—and make a total spectacle of ourselves.

I would feel bad that we're interrupting Ryder's big moment, but then again, we're both in this position because we helped hand him that moment, so I suppose he can tolerate us and our needs.

"I need a healer for him," I say, trying to get a better look at the damage and trying to ignore the pain in my own body, only exacerbated by the fall. "We need to see what can be done."

We need to learn how bad the damage is, but I don't say it out loud, like speaking it into the universe might make the damage irrevocable.

Gods, the damage that sword does—what if it really is irrevocable?

Creatures like us don't worry about that. Not after we grow into adulthood, at least. It's been nearly eight centuries since I've even thought of an injury as something permanent. They're annoying, and sometimes quite painful. They can even be a hindrance, depending how long they take to heal. But they're not permanent, not like this one will be.

Ryder motions some of his loyal soldiers towards us. I try to stand on my own, ready to help move my mate somewhere safe where he can be looked over.

Evidently, I have underestimated just how much energy I used in today's fight. The room sways, and then it feels like my body isn't quite put together right, like the world and my mind are detaching from each other.

And then, everything goes dark.

***

I wake up in my own bed, the warmth of my mate against my side.

"You're awake."

I scramble to sit up, noting absently that I feel significantly better, like the world is righted once more. But I can't dwell on the thought for long, because a demon I don't know is sitting in a chair at the foot of my bed.

"Who the fuck are you?" I demand, ready to do whatever it takes to defend us from this stranger.

"Ryder sent me as a healer." He looks bored, as if he's threatened by bed-bound patients every single day, but that doesn't mean I trust him.

"How did you get in here?" I challenge. No one should be able to enter my rooms but me and those I invite.

"The queen-mother let me in."

That stops me short. Right, the queen. Since I made her a bedroom here, Demonheim would see this chamber as hers as much as it is mine. I make a note to close her room as soon as possible. Surely, with her son on the throne, she can safely return to her old rooms, or any other arrangement of rooms that suits her, without needing to stay here.

I study the man for a long moment, trying to determine if he poses any threat to us. But I have to believe that Ryder and Hannah know where we are too, and hopefully checked anyone the queen-mother let in.

And Ryder's my king now. If he trusts this demon, then by default so do I.

"How is he doing?" I ask, daring to look away from the intruder in our bedroom to look my mate over. He looks like he's sleeping relatively peacefully. The only thing that mars the look is the bandages wrapped around his head, holding thick padding to his left eye.

"I'm unsure if he'll ever see out of that eye again," the healer admits. "I don't see many injuries like this. With creatures like us, wounds are typically either mortal, or easily healed. It's only children I worry about like this."

I've already figured as much out, but I don't interrupt. If he knows something that I don't, then I need to hear it. I need to know how to look after Heath.

"And other than his vision?" I ask.

"The bleeding stopped. There's nothing about the blade that indicates poison, or infection, or anything of that caliber to be frightened of. It just creates a limited mortality. He will recover and recover fully, other than that eye. But healing is exhausting, and so is pain. When he wakes, we can evaluate how bad the damage is." He stands. "Now that you're awake, I'll take my leave. Call me back when he's alert so we can check his eye."

I barely nod as he leaves, not caring in the least.

I run my hand through Heath's hair, careful not to move any of the bandages. Touching him, even softly like this, feels like a gentle hum beneath my skin, the energy in my body replenishing and multiplying.

When he wakes, we'll navigate whatever he needs together. We'll make plans for the future. We can do that now that we survived.

We'll have a life. Every dream I've ever wanted, everything I didn't even know I wanted until Heath came stumbling into my life—that's what we'll have.

There's a knock at the bedroom door. I grit my teeth, then slide my body around so I'm fully between Heath and the door. "Yes?"

Ryder enters. I gape at him, and he must see it on my face, because he looks sheepish. "My mother let me in," he says. "I hope you don't mind."

Mind? Of course I mind. But I school my face into an appropriate mask, not saying anything, not complaining to my king how his mother, the former queen, is turning my private sanctuary into a busy boarding house.

"How can I help you, your majesty?" I ask, trying to hide any exhaustion or growing sense that I certainly don't want company from him as he walks into the room and sits in the abandoned chair.

He raises an eyebrow. "I don't expect you to call me that."

"You should," I say before I can stop myself, even knowing how impolite it might be. "You should expect everyone to call you that. You're king now. And a new king, coming after a contentious murderer of a ruler. You should ensure everyone is reminded that you're in charge."

He smirks. "Sound advice," he agrees. "And not a your majesty in sight. I like it."

I flush. Damn him. "Your majesty," I belatedly add, sounding foolish just for saying it.

"I owe you too much to stand on ceremony with you," he continues, ignoring my fumbling attempt to correct myself.

"You owe me nothing."

I didn't do this for accolades, or recognition, or even to finally belong to the family that I have no right to, anyway. I did this because the demons of Demonheim deserved better than what they had. Anyone who could have helped would have.

"You helped protect my people. You helped rescue my mother from the cages. You passed information to my queen and I, at great personal risk. You appeased our monster of a father to gain any information you could. And you and your mate are the reason we were able to take the throne today at all. Shall I go on, listing ways I owe you, Chase?"

Somehow, with all that, the only words I am able to latch onto are our monster of a father. Our. Our.

He barely acknowledged me as a son before he tried to kill me. Queen Olette didn't acknowledge me as her husband's bastard, nor would I ever expect her to. But here stands Ryder, fresh to the throne and with everything still to lose, admitting the blood that binds us.

"You shouldn't say that," I croak. "Our father. You shouldn't admit to having a brother at all. Even if your right to rule comes from your mother and Demonheim would never recognize my blood as worthy of anything, you still shouldn't say it. Don't admit to it, don't let anyone see his line as having any possible contenders for the throne."

He's silent for a long moment, but then says, "Your existence isn't a secret, Chase."

"Not a secret and openly acknowledged by the new king are two different things," I protest. "And it's secret enough from all but a few. We can keep it a secret."

"And that wouldn't offend you?"

"You said yourself he was a monster. Not having to explicitly state my connection to him doesn't seem like such a sacrifice," I say honestly.

How many times had I wished my father was someone else, anyone else? That he was kind and generous. That he would have supported me, loved me. That I didn't have to feel any culpability of the choices and rages of a monster.

"I'm not talking about him. I'm talking about me. Your brother," Ryder says. He leans forward in his chair. "Do you know when I found out about you?"

I've always known about him, of course, since the day he was born. I was an adult, so I admit my half-brother had been little more than a curiosity. I'd known without ever asking that I'd never get to acknowledge him as a brother. I might never even get to speak to him.

This whole conversation is bizarre, and I assume it can't get any stranger. "When did you find out?"

"Hannah told me. When you became her contact inside." That recently? I shouldn't be surprised, and I shouldn't be hurt.

Like he can read the hurt on my face regardless, he says, "I want you as my brother now. The one good thing I can take from that man."

"What does that entail?" I ask hesitantly.

"Well, I planned to ask you to work as my advisor. But I have a feeling you won't be able to."

"What? Why not?" I demand, torn between being indignant at him pulling something away from me and resigned that he's seeing sense.

He raises an eyebrow. "Because a wolf could never thrive in Demonheim."

I want to argue that Heath was doing just fine before, but I don't. He did fine in my rooms, in the one domain I can control and make hospitable to him. Otherwise, he cannot leave this room without me, or else he'll get lost. And he spent ten days in the cages. No rational being would want to be near the cages again after that, I think.

"I still pledge my loyalty to you," I promise, throat feeling tight.

"I'll gladly accept. And know, wherever you go, whatever may happen—you have a home here, and a place by my side. Both of you."

He rises. "I'll get my mother settled somewhere else," he promises. "Give you and your mate a chance to rest and some peace."

I appreciate the gesture, although I don't doubt for a moment that Ryder could force his way back in here at the slightest whim. It's been a while since we've had a fully powered ruler of Demonheim on the throne, and the realm will always bow to its ruler.

Even so, the gesture is nice, because I could certainly use some peace with my mate.

Chapter Thirty-Three

Chase

When Heath wakes up, it's not a gentle waking. It's a man still in the midst of some fight in his mind, and he comes up swinging.

Fortunately, either the recent bout of unconsciousness or the poor vision limits his ability to land a hit, and I dodge his swings easily enough until I can get in his face and make him feel that it's me and we're safe here.

"Chase?" he asks after a moment, breathing heavily. He seems to be coming back to himself, but I still move slowly, just in case.

"It's me. We're okay. It's done, Heath. He's dead. Ryder took the throne. Demonheim is safe." I keep up a gentle litany of all that's happened, all the ways we're safe now.

"What the fuck happened to me?" he asks, raising one hand to his face. We pulled the bandages off yesterday, so I grab his hand before he can touch the still not fully healed wound. The healer assured me it was better for the wound to be exposed to the air at this point, and I trust him because I don't know enough to say otherwise, but I still think having a raw wound like that uncovered is terrifying.

Is this what humans live like? No wonder they're always so desperate for deals with demons. Their lives are so fragile.

I stroke my fingers over the back of his hand to try to keep him calm. "Heath, your eye—"

He stills, like he's remembering what happened. "Is it gone?"

"Not gone," I tell him. "It's just injured. We did everything we could, but the healer isn't sure if you'll ever see out of it again." I pause for a moment. "Can you...?"

I shouldn't ask, I realize as soon as I say it. It's too soon to even worry about that, and I shouldn't pressure him.

But it's too late to take my words back now. He just shakes his head. "Nothing." He tries to give me a smile. It looks shaky at best. "Good that wolves don't just rely on sight, right?"

"Yeah," I agree, running the hand not holding his through his hair and trying to match my tone to his. "That's very good, Heath."

He's silent for a moment, then asks, "Ryder took the throne? It's done?"

"It's done," I confirm. "Hannah is busy with... well, everything, from what I've heard. But I'm sure she'll make time to come talk to you, to catch you up on everything."

"I don't need Hannah," he dismisses. "She's busy with her mate and her kingdom; I can respect that. You'll tell me what's going on." He looks at me, and although his good eye focuses on me, I can't help the pang of sorrow at the sight of his mangled eye. "What is going on, Chase?"

I shrug. "I don't know much more than you, to be honest. The healer coming by is the only word I've had except for the one time Ryder came to see me. Mostly, he's been keeping people away, giving us time to recover. But from what I hear, he's making Demonheim safe to come back to. And he's making it clear that things have changed around here."

Heath nods. "And me? Us?"

"The healer will be back in the morning to check your eye. Now that you're awake, maybe he'll know more. But it's healing like a mortal would heal, Heath. So it's slow, and it won't heal perfectly."

He bites his lip, and I expect some sort of reaction, but all he does is take a breath. "Alright, then," he says, and I know that he's not ready for me to push him on this yet. But I'll need to later. This isn't alright. And he can't pretend the adjustment will be easy.

"Ryder offered you some sort of court appointment, didn't he?" he asks, changing the subject neatly from himself.

And I'm baffled that he knows that, so I let him get away with it. "Were you awake?"

"No. But it's a logical thing. Anyone can see you were instrumental in making his ascension to the throne happen. He owes it to you. More than that, he should want your support."

He says it with so much confidence, like wanting me and my advice is a foregone conclusion.

"We both decided it would be best if I didn't take it."

He sits up so fast that I'm almost knocked back. "Why not?" he growls. "Is it because of your father? Because if it is, I'll make Ryder see reason. There's no reason to deny you based on someone else's actions. He doesn't get to throw you away after all you did—all you almost sacrificed—"

I want to say that I didn't sacrifice much, and even if I did, I would have done it for Demonheim. But I think if I waste time explaining that, Heath will climb out of bed and go off to find my brother, eye or no, throne or no. So I hasten to say, "We decided it because I'm going to leave, Heath."

That doesn't settle him. "He's forcing you out?" He looks like he'd gladly pick up a sword to defend me from my brother. Perhaps his determination to fight should make me uneasy, but instead it makes something in me go soft. He'd really do it, challenge the king of Demonheim to a fight for me.

This man is something else. Something incredible, really.

"I'm going to leave with you," I tell him, catching his arm before he really does storm away to start a fight. "Because Demonheim isn't hospitable to you. You can't pretend you want to stay here."

He freezes, then the tension leaves his muscles like his strings were cut. "I'm not going to force you to leave," he mutters.

"Oh, so your sister wouldn't be upset if one of her loyal princes never returned home?" I ask. "Demonheim will always be my home, and I'd appreciate it if you didn't try to keep me away from it. If Ryder will have me, I'd love to come back and provide whatever support I can. But nothing says I have to live here."

I have no idea what life will look like outside of Demonheim. I've rarely ever left the realm before, and never for very long. But, with Heath at my side, I'm eager to find out.

Heath looks like the fight has gotten knocked out of him, and he's not necessarily happy about it. I suppose it's easier to fight than to think about what's happened. "You'll like our village," he says after a long moment.

He won't look me directly in the eye, and I don't know if it's because he somehow thinks he can avoid me seeing the damage to his left eye, or if he's trying to hide his thoughts from me.

Either way, I use my hold on his arm to tug him back to reclining on the bed, sliding in next to him so I can hold him. "Then tell me about it."

Chapter Thirty-Four

Heath

After another five days of being kept in the bedroom—and not in a fun way, but rather more like a disobedient, accident-prone child—the healer declares that my vision will only partially come back to my left eye.

The healer seems impressed that any vision at all is returning. Meanwhile, I've known for days that I can see shadowy shapes, splotches of color, and movement that looks oddly flat and stilted.

It's jarring, to realize over and over again, day after day, that I'm missing a large piece of everything going on around me. And that's when I'm just in this bedroom, where nothing truly complex is happening. I can't imagine what it will be like once I go back into the world.

Will I even be useful to the pack like this?

Celia will find a task for me, of that I'm sure. But I don't want her pity, and I don't want a job just so she can say I'm still useful. I want to do what I've always done, and be who I've always been.

Wolves might have strong senses, but that doesn't change how much information can be gathered from sight. I'm not useful to Celia like this.

Chase is the only bright point for me at this moment. Because he's alive, and we saved each other, and as far as things I'd willingly lose an eye over, saving Chase's life is at the top of my list. And because he's coming home with me. I don't delude myself into thinking it's as insignificant a decision as he's making it out to be.

He's right; I wouldn't survive Demonheim. This place simply isn't meant for me, and the proximity to the cages makes me nervous whenever I think too long about it. I'll visit with Chase whenever he wants me to, of course. But I doubt I could adapt to living here.

But that doesn't mean he'll adjust easily to life among the pack.

If he's going to make that sacrifice for me, then I want to give him everything. I'll help him find his place in the pack, and I'll show him we can provide everything he could ever desire.

I know he can provide for himself. He probably can do it easier than I can, considering his magic. But it's the wolf in me, liking to think I can bring back whatever my mate desires to our den.

All that's left is to be healthy and whole for him.

"Could demon magic heal my eye?" I ask him once the healer leaves.

He goes still. "I could try. I don't know if it'll work. That blade—the healer says all it does is make the flesh it parts mortal, and I can heal mortals, but the blade feels evil."

"Feels evil?" I ask, momentarily intrigued and distracted from my goal.

"You'd understand if magic was a part of you. I can't explain it. Magic just feels a certain way. And that blade feels evil. Like it means to do as much harm as possible with every strike."

I consider it for a moment. "I get it. It smells evil. I can't explain that to you, it just—does."

He nods, accepting that. "Right. And I don't know if I can heal that sort of magical damage."

"What's Ryder going to do with that thing, anyways?" I ask. I can't picture him using it as a tool to enforce his power like his father did.

"He wants to melt it down. Failing that, I think he'll find somewhere to hide it," Chase tells me. "Hannah is working on logistics. I don't know any more than that. I left to come back to hear what the healer had to say."

Right. Because my infirmity is keeping Chase from important council meetings. In his limited chance to be at his brother's side full-time, my needs are keeping him away. Guilt washes through me.

"Can you try to heal it?" I ask again.

"I'll try. But the energy involved..." He looks concerned. "I could exhaust myself. I'll probably exhaust you."

"It won't hurt you, right?" I check, because that's the one thing I could never abide, hurting my mate. I would take out both eyes before even contemplating it.

"It shouldn't, not permanently. That's why demons have mates—so we have the energy for this type of magic. Let's try." He sits up on his knees on the edge of the bed, then motions for me to lie back. "I'm going to be touching you the whole time. Best way to connect our energy." He lays his hands on my bare chest, then pauses. "And I need you to say it, explicitly. Contracts and all that. You know how it is."

I don't, really, but I don't question it. "I'd like you to heal my eye," I tell him. "In exchange, I give you as much energy as you need."

He sucks his teeth. "Don't ever make that type of deal with any other demon," he scolds, but he doesn't take his hands off me, and they start to feel warm. He leaves one hand on my chest, then slides the other up my neck, over my jaw, until he's covering my eye, careful not to touch the still-healing skin.

The heat increases until Chase's naturally overly-warm skin feels like it's burning. He's absolutely silent as he continues, and, as the minutes stretch out, I stare up at him with my good eye.

He looks entirely focused on his task, like every little bit of his mind is dedicated to this one thing. Sweat breaks on his brow, and his hands start to shake slightly against my skin.

Finally, with seemingly no signal that things have changed, Chase releases me. He leaves the hand on my chest, but the burning stops, and the touch becomes more gentle, almost absently affectionate. He lifts his hand from my eye. "Any difference?"

I close my good eye and look around, forcing my eye to take in first him, and then the bedroom around us. I can see him, but the edges are blurred, like I'm looking through water. I sigh. "A little better, maybe," I decide. It's a generous assessment.

He slumps slightly, and I reach up to pull him down onto me, wanting to comfort him, not wanting him to take this blame onto himself.

"We can keep trying," he says. "Not right away—one of us will pass out, and I'm tired of that healer coming into our bedroom—but in a day or so. We can try again, and see if it gets better over time."

"Will it get better?" I push. I think we both know it won't. Chase is right. That blade is evil, and the damage it does is evil.

"Won't know unless we try," Chase says, but his subtle shifting in place tells me he's no more convinced than I am.

"That was everything you have to give," I say. I'm not asking; I can feel him shaking.

"Technically, everything I have to give would be—"

"Do not finish that thought." I won't think about the consequences of him going too far. Him hurt, him dying because I was greedy and selfish.

I just need to come to terms with this. After all, I lost my eye attempting to defend my mate. A wolf can be proud of that.

I'll adjust. I have to.

"We're done," I tell him. "It didn't work. The blade's damage is as permanent as everyone always predicted. I'll live with it." I force myself to look at Chase, putting worries about my eye as far back in my mind as I can. I smile slowly, deliberately. "You don't want the healer coming by anymore, hm? Worried he'll catch us doing things in here?"

"Like anyone would be stupid enough to think two new mates aren't—you sure?" he asks, when I decide I'm done with talking and reach for his trousers instead.

"I'm sure," I promise.

And I am. I am sure. I'm sure I want Chase, that he is the best part of all of this. That I love being with him, and want to know every inch of him. And I'm sure that this will help me forget, and I'll latch onto that with both hands eagerly.

CHAPTER THIRTY-FIVE

CHASE

Heath thinks he has something to prove, and I hate it, but I also don't know how to dissuade him of that.

His eye was damaged fighting for Demonheim, while the two of us fought for our lives. He was hurt protecting me. What could he possibly have to prove to me?

Nevertheless, he's desperate to prove whatever it is. I can feel it in the way he touches me, the way he grabs me too tight, the way his mouth is desperate against mine.

And I give in.

Maybe I can prove something back. Maybe we both need this, and maybe he'll know for certain that, eye or no eye, I won't leave him behind.

This man is my mate. Nothing else matters. He is the other half of my soul, something I've been unknowingly searching for my entire life. I'm going to give up Demonheim for him and be happy about it. He's a fool if he thinks there's any world where he loses me.

So I kiss just as hard, touch just as firmly, draw him just as close.

"Tell me what you want," I demand, pulling back from sucking a bruise on his collarbone. I still have my trousers on, stuck around my knees, but I couldn't care less. I want him, and I want him now, and if he wants that too, then it's what we'll get.

"You, riding me," he says, words as firm as his fingers questing down my sides, seeking to dig into the flesh of my ass.

I don't argue, instead using magic to bring me a bottle of oil. I kick off my trousers and straddle his thighs, opening the oil and pouring some onto my hand, getting my fingers nice and slick so I can open myself for him.

I rock against him as I open myself, sliding first one finger inside me, then two, spreading them gently. His hands never leave my hips, groping and squeezing as I get ready to take him.

When I go to rub the last of the oil along his cock, I realize he's not watching me.

His head is turned away, left side lower so I can't see the damage to his eye. Like he wants me to forget it's there, perhaps.

I couldn't forget it. I don't want to forget it.

"Are you okay?" I ask, the hand that had been aiming for his cock now on his lower stomach, sprawled wide to offer comfort. I'm covering the skin there in oil, but I couldn't care less.

"I'm fine," he growls. He doesn't turn to look at me.

I frown. "Heath—"

"I'm fine," he says again, the growl becoming more pronounced. Then he turns suddenly, grabbing me by the hips and flipping me onto my back, moving so he's over me.

The move is so quick it practically winds me, but I just stare up at his face, hovering over me.

"If I wasn't fine, could I do this?" he asks. Then, using one hand for balance and one to hold his cock, he guides himself inside of me. As soon as the head is in, he slams inside up to the hilt.

I cry out. We haven't had sex in over a week, and the stretch feels good, but it's sudden, and I never expected Heath to be so reckless.

He doesn't wait, just starts quick, powerful thrusts, like he needs to prove to us both that he can. Like I ever doubted him.

I try to reach for his hair, try to gentle him with soft strokes, but my own blood is getting heated now. He's wild and reckless above me, fucking me hard and fast and impossibly deep, and it feels so. Damn. Good.

I want more, and everything in me that worries is shushed by the pleasure lighting me on fire.

So I chase my pleasure. I grab at him and rock my hips into him and moan as he pounds into me, filling me so deliciously. Maybe this is what we both need.

He leans down, resting his head against my shoulder, and I regain enough thought to worry for a moment that he's trying to hide his face again. But then he bites my neck, hard enough that I'll undoubtedly have a mark for a few hours.

"You're going to come for me," he rasps against my skin, then rubs his tongue across the mark he just left, making me shudder. "Come for me, Chase. Come around my cock. Let me feel it."

Those seem to be magic words, as compelling as any demon magic. On the next stroke, he hits that spot inside me perfectly, and I can't help it; I gasp his name, and come all over both of our stomachs.

Heath doesn't hold out, shouting my name as he comes inside me, pumping his hips hard and fast while I shudder through my orgasm until his come is overflowing my hole.

He doesn't slide out of me for a long moment, just resting his head in the crook of my neck, his lips and teeth and hands now gentle on my skin.

I return my hands to his hair, stroking gently again, returning to myself now.

Gentle. Comforting. Telling him I'm still here.

Eventually, he goes soft and slips out of me. I can feel come spilling out of me, making a mess, but I don't move to clean us up yet. Instead, I continue to hold him close.

I press a kiss to the top of his head. "Tomorrow, we'll go see Ryder," I tell him. "And let him know it's time for us to leave."

CHAPTER THIRTY-SIX

HEATH

When I wake up in the morning, the room smells like the both of us. It smells like stale sex and dried semen and sweat, and I know these scents aren't entirely pleasant, but the wolf in me is pleased to know our scents are mingled together like this.

And I wake my mate by licking him clean, exactly as my most wolfish instincts demand.

He comes, shuddering, with his hole empty of come and his cock in my mouth. His hands rake through my hair again, long, luxurious strokes with a slight scraping of his fingernails against my scalp that I'm getting irrationally attached to.

"What can I do for you?" he asks, sounding much more awake now.

I could come with just a few strokes of his hand, my hard cock having rubbed mercilessly against the sheets the entire time I buried my face against him. I place his hand on me, and fall boneless under his touch, closing my eyes against the onslaught.

Touch. Scent. Taste. The sound of Chase's soft breaths, his little pants, the way he says my name. The world still feels right to me with just these to guide me.

***

I realize belatedly as we reach the throne room that only Chase and that damned healer have seen the damage to my eye so far.

Now, everyone can see it. Ryder, Queen Olette, Hannah, a dozen courtiers, and guards. I try to hold my head high, to not flinch away from what happened.

I got this wound by winning that throne, I remind myself. I don't need to feel ashamed. Not in front of anyone here.

Everyone pretends not to see it, but I can feel their eyes on me.

"So, you're leaving," Ryder says before Chase can explain himself.

I feel a pang of regret. I've been too worried about my eye, about my future, to fully register that my concern should be with my mate, who is leaving his life behind for me.

"We are," Chase agrees, and I study him as he speaks. He seems firm in what he's saying, and I don't sense any doubt.

Gods, how do I make this worth it for him?

Ryder sits on the throne like a king, taking up space, imposing his presence on all of us. His horns look sharper, and I don't think that's just my poor vision.

Hannah has a throne now too, right next to her mate's. The mercenary I fought alongside—bled alongside, slept in the dirt alongside—looks oddly comfortable on the throne, gracefully taking up the space like she was always owed it.

"If I call you, will you come?" Ryder asks Chase, a heavy gravitas to his words that I don't fully understand.

"I will," Chase replies, voice equally serious.

"Then go in peace," Ryder says. "And know Demonheim will always welcome you home."

Chase shivers. Once again, I don't feel anything, but I'm sure that there is some sort of hidden magic of Demonheim at work here.

Ryder shakes his shoulders and stands from the throne, Hannah immediately following him. Then they both step down towards us, and I brace for what they have to say.

Ryder smiles at his brother, softer and more natural than his words a minute ago would indicate. "Demonheim will miss you," he says to him softly, then pauses a second. "I will miss you."

"You barely know me," Chase argues, but it's half-hearted at best.

Hannah claims my attention. "Returning to your pack?"

"It seems so," I tell her. "And you?"

She sighs. "Running Demonheim, it seems. No more wild adventures for me." She elbows me. "Don't think I'll start slipping, though. I'm still lethal."

Of that, I have no doubt.

"And I'll keep this one alive. Make the work you did to get us here worth it." She pauses for a moment. "Take care of that one, alright?"

"I will," I say, now looking firmly at my mate, drawn into a heated discussion with his brother. "I'll..." I trail off, not sure what to say. I want to say I'll offer him the world, welcome him to my family, make him feel things he's never felt before. I want to make a thousand promises, and then work for the rest of my life to keep them.

Hannah sighs wistfully. "Yeah," she agrees.

***

Chase brings us to the outskirts of the village.

The scent of home stops me in my tracks. I didn't realize I missed it, but as the pine and the fires and the familiar people and the fresh dirt fill my senses, I've suddenly never felt more right.

Chase clutches my hand in surprise. "It's so green," he murmurs.

I try to take it in from his perspective, from the eyes of a man who's rarely left Demonheim. I suppose the greenery, the forests and the mountains, would be unexpected.

"It is," I agree. "It's refreshing." At least, I hope Chase comes to feel that way, too. "Do you want to meet my family?"

"Will they tolerate me?" he asks. "I know demons—"

"You could be anything in the world, and it wouldn't matter," I interrupt. "You're my mate, and, for a wolf, that's everything. They'd love you just for that, for what you mean to me. But I also know they'll come to love you for you." Or at least I hope they will. We all eventually came to love Bethany, at any rate. Bethany had been a wolf and had more easily blended into our pack, but I tell myself that doesn't matter. Chase is Chase. Chase is strong, and smart, and loyal and determined, all qualities that wolves value highly.

And he's mine, and I'm his, and no wolf in their right mind would ever step between that.

"We live this way," I say, turning my head to look where our home has stood for as long as I've been alive. My father and mother laid the logs for it by hand, built every piece of furniture, and maintained it rigorously.

"Tell me about your siblings," he asks as we walk, and I think I detect a hint of nervousness.

"You waited until now to ask?" I tease.

"I just spoke to my brother, who genuinely wants to call me brother now. Forgive me for just realizing I know nothing about yours." I can smell his worry on his sweat, and think of what I can say to soothe him.

We're like any other family, I suppose, although Chase might not know very much about that. And while every one of us is capable of defending our territory and Celia's crown with our dying breaths, we're mostly normal, and gentle, and I want Chase to see that.

Whether or not he's ready to hear it, they're his family now, too. And I want him to feel at home among them.

"Celia is our queen. She's older than Bryce by a few minutes, and older than me by about an hour," I tell him. "Her mate is Bethany. Bryce is Celia's second in command. He calls himself her diplomat, but he does a lot more than that. He keeps all the pieces together." I smile softly, thinking of my siblings. "And he always looks like he's angry for having to do it. The youngest is Callum. He's fifty years younger than us."

"That must have been hard," Chase comments.

I shrug. "Not unusual for wolves to keep having children whenever they manage it. I would assume that we would have had a half dozen more siblings over the years, if my parents had lived long enough. Callum wasn't even twenty yet when they died, though. Practically a child, and no new siblings yet after him."

Callum had been young, but then again, so had we all. Celia had been too young when the future of all wolves was placed on her.

Even I can see the home over the hill now, but I've been chasing the scent of it the entire time. I can smell my family, the fire, the meal Bethany has no doubt made for dinner, the herbs and flowers used to keep the house fresh.

Chase takes my hand and squeezes. "Anything I should know? To make them like me?"

I might feel like I'm home, like the very scent of this house is a warm hug, but I know that feeling is entirely foreign to Chase. His chambers in

Demonheim are probably the closest he ever had, and I've always felt that he valued them more for security than any sense of belonging.

But I'll give him a place here. I will show him that he can belong here, that he can love this village. That he can love us.

People spill out of my home, heartbeats and pounding feet paired with the blurry images I can see. "Heath?"

That's my sister. I catch her when she throws herself at me, accidentally pulling Chase's hand, still clasped in mine, into the hug. With my free hand, I hold the back of her head.

"You're back," she murmurs, voice muffled by my shoulder. "And you brought someone."

Leave it to wolves to turn right to that. We always put our mates above all, and a new mate in the family is something deserving of celebration. Something deserving forgiveness too, probably, so I'm likely to get away with however mad my leaving made them.

There's nothing I would rather discuss than my mate. Even after everything that happened, he still comes first in my mind.

"This is Chase," I say to her, although I'm well aware that my brothers and Bethany can easily hear us. "My mate. He saved my life."

Chase makes a noise of protest. "You saved mine."

Celia laughs, a little broken, a little relieved. "It seems you have a story."

I let her go when she starts pulling away, and I can't miss her sharp intake of breath when she sees my face for the first time. "A long story, probably," she surmises.

She's not wrong. "Let's talk inside."

Chapter Thirty-Seven

Chase

I'm welcomed into the family home, a sprawling lodge that seems to be mostly one open room, with a loft above and some smaller rooms in the back. Presumably, those are the rooms the siblings sleep in.

Where I'll sleep now, I realize. Because this is my home, or at least where I live. I'm not quite sure if it qualifies as my home yet, and it feels presumptuous to say so, particularly since everyone here is gaping at me.

Celia eyes me speculatively. Far from the emotional display outside, she has adopted a cool, reserved, calculating posture as she watches us.

"Chase," she says, and it doesn't sound like either a question or an invitation to speak. I just nod instead.

Heath squeezes my hand again. "I went to Demonheim," he tells them.

One of the brothers—tall, dark, and brooding, with shorter hair than Heath—rolls his eyes. "Clearly."

"Demonheim has a new king," he continues as if his brother never spoke. "Chase and I ensured it."

The brother farthest in the back raises an eyebrow. "You did that?"

I squeeze Heath's hand. Maybe it's the reminder that we are responsible for changing the tide of the war in Demonheim. Maybe it's simply the need to defend my bond with my mate. Either way, I no longer feel the need to be welcomed before I speak.

"Heath saved me," I tell them. "Again and again. He went to the cages to save me."

That stops everyone in the room, chilling the air. Everyone has heard the rumors of what the cages are. Heath doesn't look inclined to confirm or deny the rumors, though. "Chase saved me right back," he simply says. "We make a good team."

The brother who rolled his eyes a moment ago looks at our clasped hands. "Congratulations to you both," he says, radiating sincerity despite the still rather dour expression. "What can you tell me about the new king?"

Bryce then, I conclude. The brother who acts as the wolves' diplomat, already thinking about the larger implications of what has changed.

I wonder absently if he's ever met my father. I doubt it—demons are notoriously withdrawn, and with our own realm to hide away in, very few feel the need to send ambassadors to us—but I suppose it's possible.

"Ryder is Chase's brother," Heath informs him.

"Didn't want to make a play for the throne yourself?" The other brother, who must be Callum, asks.

I startle, unable to answer for a second as I parse the ridiculous question. "I have no claim on the throne."

"Then how—ah." I half wonder about how happy and secure their parents' bond must have been, for the thought of infidelity and secret children to be a shock to them.

The tall, willowy woman with nearly white hair smiles at me. "We want to welcome you to our home, Chase," she says. "I'm Bethany. And everyone here will have the manners to introduce themselves."

I don't tell her that I've already guessed who everyone is as they go around and confirm it.

"There's food," Bethany says once Callum gives his name. "I imagine you must be hungry after such a long journey."

"Not so long," Heath says, tugging gently on my hand to pull me near to a long table. "Chase's magic is pretty impressive."

I wait for some sort of fear reaction, or some sort of anger. I'm not deluded into thinking demon magic is something people desire in their home. While we can't force people to enter our deals, people nevertheless fear them, and, as a result, shun us.

The horns on my head might as well be a beacon, telling them to stay away, and Heath might have just reminded them of that.

I try to save the conversation, offering a smile that I hope shows I mean no harm. "It can be exhausting regardless. I would appreciate a meal."

Bethany smiles again, and if it's less sincere than the first one, she does a good job of hiding it. "Of course." She motions for everyone to follow her.

Callum helps Bethany bring food to the table, setting bowls in front of all of us. "So, when do we talk about the eye?" Celia asks, squeezing her mate's hip in thanks for her food, and looking directly at her brother.

There's no beating around the bush here. I suddenly have a vision of who Ryder might be in a century or two. The firm, no-nonsense persona a too-young monarch might need to take.

Heath shrugs. "I took a slice from that damned sword."

"He was trying to protect me," I interject, because it seems important for them to know that.

"I can see enough." Heath says it before letting them ask anything else about the incident, like he has to get it out. The response is firm and doesn't invite further questions, and I fight not to react, because I know for a fact that his vision is certainly impaired.

Well, I certainly won't be the one to nay say him, even if I think lying to his family is a stupid move. Then again, what do I know about having a family?

Chapter Thirty-Eight

Heath

Sometime after the meal, I feign tiredness so we can retreat to my room.

I am tired, but only of needing to keep up an act around my family. I've never needed to do that before.

Oh, we've had petty sibling squabbles, moments of pride and hurt feelings. We all tried unsuccessfully to protect each other from our grief after our parents were killed. But I don't think I've ever truly hid something from them before, because at the end of the day, we always know we can rely on each other.

While that may be true still, I don't need them to know any more about my eye, or the cages, or anything else. I have a role in this family, after all. And I can't suddenly be unable to fill it.

Not just for them. For me, too; I can't be the link that breaks. We are strong because we're the four Crae siblings, and us three brothers stand strong behind Celia, keeping the pack together. I can't suddenly fail them at that. I can't give them a reason to worry.

There's a much less insidious reason I want to retreat to my room, of course; I want a moment to hold my mate.

Today's been hard on him. I'm not so distracted by my own worries that I miss that. While he willingly offered to come here, I can't pretend what we're doing is at all easy on him.

But it seems even the peaceful night comforting my mate that I envisioned isn't to be. "Why did you lie to them?" he asks me almost as soon as the door is shut.

"Keep your voice down," I say, firm and quiet. "They're wolves. They can hear you."

He snorts, a bitter laugh that I find I hate. "You think they can't already tell? I don't even know them yet and even I know that you didn't convince a single person at that table that you're alright."

"I'm fine."

"They're your family," he stresses, now keeping his voice lower. "And I might not know much about that, but they're supposed to support you, love you, help you. Right?"

He takes a step, drawing close to me but hesitating to touch me. I sigh and take him into my arms. It's not him I'm mad at, and I know it.

"I'm not ready to deal with their reactions," I tell him. "If they're worried, or sad, or anything. I just need it to be just you and me right now, alright?"

He's silent for a long moment, and I worry he's going to tell me it's not alright. I have no idea what he would do in that circumstance, but even in the limited time I've known Chase, I've learned that he's crafty and clever. I'm sure I'd regret crossing him.

"Alright," he agrees. "For now."

***

The next day dawns bright and clear, the air crisp but not unbearably cold. Of course, wolves handle cold far better than most other species, and, from sleeping next to Chase, I've learned demons are like stoves, so the cold really wouldn't bother either of us.

That's good, I suppose. It can get incredibly cold here, and the house my parents built so long ago does only so much to keep out the worst of the chill.

So I take Chase on a tour of our village, showing him his way around. I show him everything from the well to the training grounds to the forest and hills surrounding the village.

The only thing I avoid is the people. When we have to pass them as we move through the town, I turn my head, as if that will keep them from seeing the travesty that is my eye. Chase squeezes my hand every time.

"Tell me about growing up here," he asks as we come across the fifth or sixth person. I know what he's doing, but I can't find it in myself to protest.

"What do you want to know?" I ask.

He's silent for a long minute. "Demonheim wasn't a bad place to grow up," he says. "And I'm certainly not the only demon to not know their father. But it was lonely. Because I did know who my father was, and I knew it was a secret that kept others away from me. And at the same time, I knew he was evaluating me for being someone he might eventually use, and I knew I fell short. And that was my entire world, Heath. So, tell me what makes this village a home."

What do I tell him? I scramble, thinking about six hundred years of memories. Over there is where Bryce and I wrestled and I hit my face on a stump—long gone now—and was left with two missing baby teeth and a bruised face. Over there is where we taught Callum his very first moves with a sword, and over there is where we fought the first time Callum put me on my ass. Celia was crowned under that big old willow tree, grief still staining the world a washed-out gray as the crown was placed on her stalwart head. My parents used to take us on picnics on the hill beyond the house.

As memories occur to me, I share them with Chase, a messy, disjointed stream of thought, pointing and walking and getting distracted by new sights. But Chase doesn't interrupt, just squeezing my hand intermittently and listening as I spill out a lifetime worth of memories. A lifetime worth of home, really.

And I hope it's enough to convince him to make his home here as well.

CHAPTER THIRTY-NINE

CHASE

This place is like nothing I've ever known.

The greenery, the freshness in the air, the openness—Demonheim is primarily corridors and passageways, and I don't think I've ever seen so much open sky before.

I'm getting used to it, but I admit it feels better when Heath is by my side. I'm quite capable of protecting myself, I like to think, so it's not that I think he's going to save me from anything. But there's a feeling like I'm less alone, less small in this too-big world when he's next to me.

Thankfully, the mating bond means neither of us will leave the other alone for too long. We explore Heath's home side-by-side, eat sitting next to each other, and sleep in the same bed. Barely a moment goes by when we don't have each other within arm's reach.

New mates are like that, Bethany tells me with a sly smirk over dinner one night. I flush at the insinuation—not an incorrect one, and sound travels through the home enough that I'm sure they all know—but don't contradict her.

It's like we're two forces who are compelled by each other, finding happiness only when we can steal moments of it together.

Because I don't fool myself into thinking either of us are truly happy. There's a grim pallor that hangs over everything but the most intimate moments between us, and even as Heath refuses to talk about it, I can't stop thinking about it.

Heath isn't himself. He's avoiding everyone, including his siblings, and I know he's using me to help him do it. And if I could stay away from him for more than a few minutes, then I'd try to force him to confront the problem. But as it is, I just keep becoming his convenient excuse.

And as for me, I'm very well aware that this isn't my home.

At breakfast on the fifth day, Bryce clasps a hand on my shoulder, which causes Heath to bare his teeth.

I don't think the brothers would really fight, not over something so stupid—I know the new mating bond can be aggressive, but Heath surely isn't impaired enough to think his brother actually wants to make a pass at me—but the growl Heath emits is chilling.

Bryce only laughs slightly. "You're with me today," he says to me, ignoring his brother entirely until he looks up and says, "Consider this payback for what we all heard last night."

Was that when I made Heath come with just my tongue, or when he fucked me so slow and sure that I wanted to cry with desperation? Either way, I want to go hide in our bedroom.

Of course, it could also have been Heath's nightmare, but we're all pretending those don't exist.

Heath doesn't so much as twitch. "You all already knew this house allows you to hear everything," he says. "Don't blame us. You're not taking him."

"You act like I plan to take him to war. I just want to speak with him about Demonheim."

"I'm right here," I remind them both, because I'd rather not be spoken about like an object for them to pass back and forth between them. "I'll talk to you. No need to take me away from Heath, though."

Callum speaks up, mouth half full of food. "Sorry, but I'm taking him from you, Chase. He hasn't put in hours on the training ground in too long, and every single soldier has more than noticed."

My hand tightens on my knife reflexively. His damn eye. I know he can fight still—his fight against my father is proof enough—but how will he react, to be asked to put that weakness on display?

He'll barely acknowledge the eye with me, never mind a whole company of wolves. He's avoided it the entire time we've been here, and now Callum wants to practically put his new weakness on display?

But I don't see how he's going to get out of his brothers' scheming without losing face, or without having to admit what he's so afraid to tell them.

It's foolish; they're his family. They're meant to accept him and love him and support him, and everything about the wolves, everything I have seen so far, tells me that those ideals of family are not mere words to them. Everything I hear about their love as siblings, their bond through the years, and the love they watched their parents have tells me his siblings would accept him through anything and go to the ends of the earth for him.

But then again, what do I know about families? I can't call myself an expert, not by any stretch of the imagination.

I see the struggle on his face as his brain frantically turns over plans, but short of running away and avoiding the entire thing, I don't think he can find a way out of it. And running away would be just as obvious a sign of struggle as going will be.

"You have until noon," he growls, menace underlying his words. Once again, his brothers barely react to the perceived threat.

In the ensuing silence, I hear a high-pitched moan from the loft above us, quickly cut off, then followed by a suppressed giggle. I wince, as does everyone else around the table.

Clearly, Celia and Bethany have their own plans for this morning, and suddenly being anywhere else seems like an excellent plan.

***

Bryce wants to meet outside. He walks at a leisurely pace, and I fall in beside him.

"Our closest neighbors, besides the humans, are the sirens to the north," Bryce says conversationally, as if I asked. "So I spend most of my time addressing those two groups. But it's my business to know a little of everything about everyone, so I want whatever you'll tell me about Demonheim."

I eye him, trying to feel out any deeper motivations. "I don't know secrets," I warn him, although that's not entirely true. "And Ryder is still my king." It's a statement and a warning. I have no intention of betraying Demonheim, regardless of who my mate is.

Bryce just waves away my concerns. "I said whatever you'll tell me, and I meant it," he promises. "You decide what I have a right to know. Although if it helps, I'm not planning an invasion. If I was, you'd be talking to your mate about it, not me. I'm a diplomat; I just want to know how to work best with the new king."

I'm sure it's more complicated than that, but I'm also sure he's sincere enough. "Ryder is being advised by his mate, Hannah, and his mother," I tell him.

He raises an eyebrow. "We presumed the queen was dead."

"Everyone did. I believed it, most everyone I know believed it, even Ryder believed it. But she spent four years in the cages."

I'm unsure if I should give him that information, but part of me feels compelled to. I doubt it can hurt anyone, what with her not being the queen anymore.

I wonder if he's going to ask me about Heath's experience in the cages now, taking advantage of the conversation. What do I tell him? I genuinely think his family might be able to help him, but I don't want to betray his trust.

Bryce doesn't ask, though. Maybe he knows it's not my right to give him any information about that. Maybe he knows that I simply don't have the answers; every piece of that horrifying experience is entirely in Heath's head.

"And why is she not on the throne?"

"Four years in the cages. Anyone would want some peace after that," I say evasively, not willing to admit my former queen is only lucid half the time.

I believe Bryce won't betray my trust, mostly because a wolf would betray a brother's mate only in the most extraordinary circumstances.

Nevertheless, I'm reluctant to share Queen Olette's weakness. She deserves the privacy she can get, and if she and Ryder and Hannah can hide it from the world, then maybe the better for her.

And I'm concerned about what conclusions they'd draw about Heath, too.

"So there's a new king," Bryce says, continuing as if what I told him was a satisfying answer. "A young king. Untested."

"He won his throne back," I point out.

"True. But as for actual governing..." He shrugs. "Who knows?"

I want to speak for Ryder, but I don't know any more than Bryce does. "He wants the best for Demonheim."

It's a weak argument, because who is to say what the best is? But Bryce accepts it with a nod.

"Tell me about courtiers. Court policy and procedures. Whatever you'd be willing to share so I can communicate with your new king and hopefully avoid looking like a fool."

Well, that I can give him, so I start thinking through policy, start telling him what I know of Ryder's personality and tastes and preferences.

Maybe there can be more than just a truce of avoidance between the wolves and the demons. Maybe we can actually create an alliance.

And maybe I can help bring it about.

CHAPTER FORTY

HEATH

When Callum hands me a sword, I know today will be bad.

"Where's *my* sword?" I grouse, acting like I actually care about the specific blade in my hand. Maybe he'll believe it. Maybe it'll buy me some time.

"It's not my job to keep track of your things," he says to me, and I remember saying the same thing to a Callum with still too-gangly limbs several centuries ago. He even somehow manages to mimic the tone, too.

"Fine," I concede, feeling the weight of the sword in my hand. "What exactly are you looking for today?"

He doesn't answer. Instead, he swings at me, and it's all I can do to block his strike.

"I thought you just came from battle," Callum taunts.

I grit my teeth. I know he's provoking me. We've done it before, all of us have. Opponents on the battlefield don't worry about your sensibilities, and we've provoked each other past the point of rage a thousand times on this training field.

I parry his next strike, noting with some grim success that I can do so even when the image in front of me seems ever so slightly distorted, too flat and not fully clear. I suppose centuries of practice means I always know where to put my blade.

It's still clumsy, though. I barely manage to parry, and by then Callum is already moving to strike again, and I'm felt feeling like I'm always two steps behind.

"You want to talk about it?" Callum asks, trying to cover for a sneaky kick to my knee that I barely dodge.

"Talk about what?" I grunt.

"We can start with that eye," he says, blunt as always. That's Callum, always the hammer, no matter the situation. He's a good man, but subtlety has never been a skill of his.

"The eye is fine." A lie. A complete, utter lie, and one Callum no doubt can see through easily. No one watching me fight right now would assume my eye is fine.

I did just fine against the king, I remind myself furiously. I'd been sure-footed and fast, and hadn't faltered even as blood dripped from my fresh wound. I'd hurt so badly, and could barely see a thing. And yet I'd struck true.

But here I am, acting like I'm being trained for the first time today.

"Can you see out of it at all?"

"Yes." I thrust to punctuate the word, and he dodges easily.

Callum slows his strikes, blocking my blows without issue and ignoring my desperation. I'm already breathing heavily—I might have taught Callum most everything I knew, but the bastard sadly perfected it from there and backs it up with a mean, powerful swing—and I know Callum will keep going all day, waiting me out.

"Not well," I eventually admit, giving in to the inevitable. "But I'm figuring it out."

Because Callum is not going to be the one who takes away my place here. As well-meaning as I'm sure this little challenge of his is, I'd be a fool to think that he's not reporting back to Celia on my every move.

It's amazing how paying back any debt I owed Hannah spiraled into this. It's not that I thought the invasion of Demonheim would be easy, or that I was invulnerable; I've been hurt plenty of times before, and I've faced hard work.

But this is exactly why that sword held such power; creatures like us know nothing about permanence.

Wolf parents turn into anxious messes over childhood illnesses even mortal children survive, because we are so far away from permanent consequences as adults. A childhood illness being able to maim or kill a child is so terrifying to us because nothing matters as adults. I've been run through on an enemy's sword and walked the next day. The idea of a sword being able to permanently alter the course of my life is mind-boggling.

But I need my siblings to know it's nothing serious. That I'm still me, and this is just a little change. It won't stop me.

It can't stop me. I won't let it.

Deep in my thoughts, I lose track of the movement around me, and Callum knocks my sword from my hand.

I stand there for a moment, stunned, the shock reverberating up my arm as I'm unable to look into my brother's eyes.

Shit.

I don't know how to recover, or how to save face. So, I walk away.

***

Chase is a smart man, and he knows something is wrong with me the moment he enters our room.

Thankfully, he has the kindness not to ask me about it right there. We truly do need to consider our own home, or else become accustomed to sneaking off into the woods every time we want to speak privately.

"Your brother told me something interesting today," he says, lying back on the mattress, still fully dressed.

"Oh?" I ask, sitting next to him. I'm glad he had a good day with Bryce, at least. I want Chase to like being here, and liking my siblings is a part of that. Even if some irrational part of me is still irritated that my brothers would dare separate us.

"After he grilled me for information about Demonheim's courtly protocols for three hours, he reminded me that we're mere days away from the full moon."

I freeze, thinking about it. Bryce is right, and I can feel it now that I'm thinking about it, wherever deep inside that the wolf roams. The full moon is coming quickly.

I hadn't felt its pull in Demonheim, a completely separate realm without any moon. If my math is right, I was in the cages the last time the full moon rose, and therefore completely cut off from feeling my own skin, let alone the moon.

Unmated wolves aren't incredibly pleasant to be around during the full moon, but we hold our rationality. Mated wolves, though?

If everything I've heard is to be believed, then it'll feel overwhelming. The single thought occupying my whole mind will be Chase, to touch and taste and fuck him. I'll be desperate for him, aching and needy and ready to chase him to the ends of the earth.

We're animals on the full moon, ready to chase and rut and fuck in the dirt. It'll be the closest the wolf inside me and I have come to each other since I managed to force the wolf back after the cages.

"Did he tell you what to expect?" I ask, torn between wanting Chase to already know and wanting to kill my brother for discussing sex with my mate without me involved.

"I know the basics," he says, which I think means no.

I lie down on the bed next to him, heedless of the clothes still between us, and pull him tight to me.

"The moon cannot make me any more obsessed with you than I already am," I tell him, pitching my voice low for his ears only. I hope it comes across as a promise. I hope he trusts my promises.

He takes my hand that's resting on his stomach and squeezes. "The moon won't change my obsession with you, either," he says.

He means it won't scare him away. I believe him, too, because after all we've been through—after plotting insurrection and the cages and almost dying together—I doubt the moon would be the thing to break us. But I also know that the intensity of wolves under the moon has been too much for many people before.

"It'll be intense," I warn him, despite his promise. Maybe because it's the right thing to do. Maybe because I want to see if he'll balk.

He squeezes my hand again. "Every day since we met has been intense. This will be much more pleasant."

I can't suppress the smile I hide against his neck. He's not wrong.

In two days, I'm going to fuck my mate under the moonlight, with nothing between us and the sky. I'm going to give him everything I have, every moment of passion, every inch of pleasure.

Chase turns in my arms until I'm looking him in the eyes, practically cross-eyed from how close he is.

"I'm going back to meet with Bryce again tomorrow," he says, a very sharp departure from what I expected from him, lying this close together in bed.

"Oh?" I ask, shifting my focus to whatever he wants to talk about, even if it takes me a moment to get my body on board with the change of topic.

"If I can help him, then I'll do it. I can't tell him everything about Demonheim, obviously, but anything I can tell him, I happily will. And I think your family has been nice to me, but when I'm working with Bryce, it feels like I'm needed here. And I've never been needed anywhere, Heath."

"You were needed in Demonheim," I disagree. I shouldn't, because I should want him to feel that this village is the best place for him, that we are the only home for him. But I can't bear to hear him disparaging himself.

He shrugs. "During the war, maybe. But not forever. I can't advise Ryder better than someone else can. I don't contribute anything to the realm. And I live here now, so that's a moot point, anyways."

The surety with which he says that he lives here is astounding and makes my heart ache in the best way.

"So, I'll be working with Bryce tomorrow. And I think you should go back to see Callum again."

"What? Why?" My failed fight practice had almost fallen from my mind.

"Because I think you need it," he says, and that's a bitter pill to swallow.

CHAPTER FORTY-ONE

CHASE

I spend the next day with Bryce, and I assume I'll spend the day with him before the moon rises. However, after breakfast, when Heath reluctantly follows Callum to the training grounds again, Celia stops me.

"You should probably do some training too," she says.

I raise an eyebrow at the implied question, the judgment, hidden under her tone, and take all the light out of the great room around us. Bryce curses.

I let the lights return, feeling decidedly sapped of energy without my mate around to draw from. I couldn't stand on the training field right now if I wanted to, but I do my best not to show it, smiling at Celia expectantly.

She shrugs, like I didn't manage to impress her, and I muster up a half-hearted offense to that. "Bryce will manage without you this morning," she says. "You're with me."

I know better than to argue with a queen. She doesn't wear a crown, I've never seen her on a throne, and she doesn't put on any airs of royalty. Still, she has a regal bearing that is inarguable, and I follow her when she leads me away from the table.

She leads me towards the bedrooms, then further back to a room she seems to conduct business out of. "Have a seat," she says, and I take one of the chairs.

She doesn't sit like a queen, or at least not my memories of Queen Olette on the throne. She sits like her brothers, sprawled out and casual, and I wonder if this is her default state, or if perhaps she trusts me enough to be less formal.

"Is my brother recovering?"

I didn't expect that question. I don't know what I expected, honestly. Maybe questions about how I fit into the pack, and what I could do for them. But I didn't expect this, and I have to scramble to think about how to talk about Heath with her. "Heath is doing everything he can," I say evasively.

"You think I don't know my brother? Heath expects his problems to fade into the shadows as easily as he does, as if we don't notice them. But I have a suspicion that won't work this time." She levels me with a piercing look. "It's bad this time, isn't it?"

I consider for a moment. "It's not good," I agree. I don't want to share things Heath doesn't want known, but Celia is both his sister and queen, so I suppose she's entitled to a certain amount of information. "Demonheim is a harsh place, especially for outsiders. And with a hostile king on the throne... you have to understand, Demonheim isn't like here. You might be queen, and your subjects might obey you. But there, the entire realm is at the whim of the monarch. And it wasn't hospitable to Heath."

"He went into the cages."

"For ten days," I agree.

"Is that something he can come back from?"

I hear the thinly veiled desperation. Will he come back from it? Will I get my brother back, exactly like he was?

"He won't be the same, probably," I admit, because I doubt anyone could be the same. The cages aren't meant to return people at all, never mind in good condition. And I didn't know him before, not really, so I don't have a great basis for comparison. But I also know that he's strong and brave, and it will probably just take time.

"And that, paired with the eye..." she trails off.

"He was able to take that sword from the king with fresh blood still dripping from his eye," I counter, a little heat entering my voice at the thought of her dismissing him. "He said it was because wolves don't rely on sight. Give him time to adjust. And anyways, his eye seems better than it was. He can see shapes and colors. He just says they're flat, like the dimensions are wrong."

"Not ideal," she muses. "But he's right; wolves have far more than sight to rely on. It's why I told Callum to force him to train. Heath's always been talented there. He taught Callum more than any of us, and the student might have long ago become the master, but hopefully he can remind Heath of why he loves it, what he's capable of."

I've been hoping that the training sessions would do that, too. So far, they've seemed to frustrate him, but they've practically just started.

She exhales slowly, slumping further back into her chair. "We just want him to be home," she says. "All four of us. He's here, but I think he's still there, sometimes. He's done plenty of hard things before, Chase. Wars. Battles. He's acted as a soldier, a spy, and even an assassin. But I've never felt like he didn't truly come home at the end before."

"Just give him a few days," I plead. "Tonight's the full moon. We've been talking about the moon."

The moon cannot make me any more obsessed with you than I already am. I can't stop thinking about that. I hope I don't blush in front of the queen.

"That's a good sign, at least," she says. Then, "Of course I'll give you two all the time in the world. There isn't a deadline; he's my brother and we love him. We'll take him in any form, however he comes to us. We want him. I just wish..."

She wishes she could help. She wishes she could wave her hand and have Heath be fine. As do I, and it's difficult to swallow that we can't.

"I know," I say. Then, again, "He'll get there."

At least, I sincerely hope so.

***

Heath's nervous energy seems to multiply as moonrise nears.

He takes me outside, walking away from the village and into the trees with purpose. The towering, ancient pines seem to swallow us whole as we go deeper in, the setting sun casting long, strange shadows through the gaps in the trees.

I've so rarely been in the world outside of Demonheim, but even I know it's unnaturally quiet out here, just our footfalls echoing and not a single animal sound. They don't like it here. Too many predators.

Finally, when we're well away and, as near as I can determine, completely alone, he takes me by the shoulders and turns me to face him.

"A full moon brings our more wolfish sides to the forefront," he says. I nod, because I know that much. "My wolf has been very close to the surface recently," he says evasively, then takes a deep, steadying breath, seeming to find the courage to say what he feels needs to be said. "Despite being called wolves, we're not supposed to actually turn into the animal," he continues. "The fact that I did in the cages is concerning. And it's rare for it to happen, so I confess I don't know what happens next. If the moon being close weakens my likely already fragile barriers, and I fall into the wolf again, I don't know..."

I sincerely doubt it will happen. After all, there's nothing here that the wolf would need to protect him against, and I like to imagine the two of us will do just fine at satiating what the wolf really wants on the full moon.

But I don't get a chance to reassure him, because he's already speaking. "If I turn, you need to disappear. Go to Demonheim, maybe, since there's no possible way for me to follow you there. Don't negotiate with the wolf, don't wait around."

"The wolf likes me," I protest. "You said so yourself."

"The wolf adores you," he corrects. "The wolf lives and dies for you, worships you. And it's also a wolf, Chase, under the full moon, where any reasoning or control I have is weakest. I don't know what it will do in the name of that adoration. And I don't mean to find out. Promise me."

I can't and won't make that promise. The wolf won't hurt me, and I won't leave Heath.

Heath's eyes, intently and desperately staring into mine, suddenly change, darkening with a feverish intensity, pupils blowing wide. At the same time, his breath comes in shorter, and his hands on my shoulder turn to a loving caress.

Moonrise is here.

CHAPTER FORTY-TWO

CHASE

"Hi, there," I say nonsensically as his hands trail from my shoulders up my neck, to finally cup my face. "We should have talked about what you wanted tonight," I mutter, more to myself than him.

His hands grope at my face, like he has to touch every inch, like he needs to memorize how I feel. Then he reaches my horns, fondling them suggestively until my knees buckle.

"Fuck, that's—that's nice," I murmur. Nice is an understatement. Nice just happens to be the most descriptive word I can muster, what with all the blood in my body going to my cock.

Heath's hands keep stroking my horns, but he buries his face in my neck, licking and sucking interspersed with long, obvious bouts of scenting me.

And when I feel the inside of my trousers becoming sticky with pre-come, Heath takes a loud, obvious sniff, then releases my horns.

I'm about to complain—I could have came from that—but he immediately drops to his knees, nuzzling against my crotch before he starts pawing at my trousers, clearly wanting them off but not quite possessing the coordination to make it happen just yet.

It's my turn to get my hands in his hair, stroking my fingers through it before I tug a little, trying to pull him away enough that I can remove my own trousers.

"I got you," I tell him, removing the rest of my clothing for good measure. I don't know why we even left them on this long. I'd rather avoid ripping one of the limited sets of clothing I possess, so I take it off and toss the pieces aside in the woods. "You next?"

I'd like to see him naked, and right now I think he'd be more comfortable. But he ignores me, instead burying his face between my thighs. He starts rather aimlessly, licking and sucking at the skin of my inner thighs. It tickles, and I'm about to tell him to stop when he kisses my balls, then sucks lightly at them.

Fuck. I look around frantically for something to lean against to keep me upright, but Heath started this in a clearing, and I have a suspicion that, in his current condition, he wouldn't be very understanding about me moving away from him to find a tree to lean against.

I put my hands in his hair again, desperate for something to hold on to. I'm tugging, but, judging by the groan that makes my cock vibrate and my legs shake, he doesn't mind being the one thing in the world holding me upright.

"You'll be the death of me," I warn him when he sucks the tip of my cock into his mouth.

He doesn't pull off to reply, not that I expected him to. Instead, he just continues to suck, to bury himself as close to my skin as he can get.

I laugh, tugging lightly on his hair. "This the wolfish side you were so worried about?" I tease. Wolves are obsessed with scent, as he's told me time and time again. And it looks like his wolfish side just wants to bury his nose in my scent as much as possible.

I already knew that Heath never gives himself enough credit, and that his worries about the wolf were more than foolish. I scratch my nails through his hair, hoping to convey that he should relax.

He doesn't look up, but he does bite at my thigh, and he's none too gentle about it, leaving a stinging mark that I'm sure will last for hours. "Okay, okay, no teasing, I get it," I laugh lightly, tugging at his hair again. "I'll let it go. For now."

He sucks my cock deep into his mouth in response, until I hit the back of his throat. I get the message loud and clear, even as blinded by pleasure as I am. Let me have my way, and I'll make you feel things you'll never feel anywhere else.

"For now," I reiterate, voice breathless now from his ministrations. He begins sucking in earnest, setting a punishing rhythm. After his fondling of my horns, I can't resist, falling closer and closer to that edge with every skillful flick of his tongue, every time his throat tightens around me.

"What about you?" I ask, forcing the words out between moans.

In response, he grabs my hips, pulling me even tighter to him, like I would ever have left, like he needs to convince me to stay.

My orgasm is inevitable, a force crashing down on me that I couldn't stop even if I wanted to. I grab his head tight, unable to resist holding him to me as I lose total control of myself and spill down his throat.

When I come back to myself, I have to try to put distance between us, because Heath is still between my legs, his tongue licking up every drop of come he can possibly find. Like a dying man in a desert, Heath seeks what he wants with single-minded determination.

I push him away, over-sensitive and wrung-out for the moment, then take a step backwards to emphasize the point.

Heath glares up at me, not like he's truly angry, but like I've stolen something from him and he doesn't understand why. His eyes are fuzzy, unclear, and I doubt he could speak to answer any questions that I might have right now. He's delirious, between the sex and the power of the moon, and I realize what it means now to be adored by his wolfish nature.

It's going to be a long night. An exhausting, highly enjoyable, very long night.

Like he can read my every thought, Heath leans up towards me, pressing little licking kisses across my belly before finally standing. I pull him into a kiss that he eagerly returns, the two of us desperate for each other out here under the moonlight.

I can taste myself on his tongue. At first I try to ignore it—my own come isn't a taste I'm particularly interested in experiencing—but it's inescapable, and soon I find myself accepting it. Heath is entirely driven by tastes and smells right now, and some part of me likes sharing this with him.

I want to taste him. I want to give him what he's given to me, make him melt with pleasure tonight. He's still fully dressed, so I start tugging at his clothes without breaking the kiss.

He seems disinterested in helping me, not giving me any room to work with. It's like he can't bear to be separated from me for even a moment, and he actually growls at me when I push at his chest to hopefully create some space.

"Heath, I need to—"

He cuts me off with yet another kiss, his tongue driving into my mouth like he's desperate, hungry. I get his trousers pushed down slightly, but he entirely ignores my efforts.

I break the kiss, turning my head slightly. "I want your cock," I tell him, trying to sound as firm as I can, trying to make my point clear. But he seemingly doesn't hear me, pressing sloppy kisses against the side of my face.

And then he herds me backwards, like he really is some sort of wolf and I'm his prey he's backing into a corner. Maybe it does make me some dumb prey animal, but I go easily enough.

He breaks the kiss to look at me, an intense stare made only more intense by the twisting scar through his eye. I briefly wonder how much he can see, if being this close helps with the odd flatness he's been describing to me, but then the thought entirely slips my mind when he grabs my hips hard enough to leave bruises for later and steers me towards something.

And then we stop. "Down," he commands, his voice an unrecognizably deep growl. And that's all he says. Not an explanation or a please, just an expectation.

But I don't argue. Just a minute ago, I was happily ready and willing to suck his cock, and who am I to quibble about where he wants it done? I sink to my knees, briefly noting the soft, mossy ground that he must have picked to bring me to. I feel a rush of warm affection that, even in this state, even desperate and driven by the moon and the wolf as he is, he'd think of something like that. Then, with soft moss under my bare knees, I look up at him expectantly.

Except he doesn't want me on my knees to suck his cock. Instead, he follows me to the ground, kneeling beside me before he gets his hands on me, pushing and steering until I get the message and go to my hands and knees, right here in the middle of the forest.

Well, they say wolves fuck and rut like animals during the full moon. He's behind me now, hands on my hips, stroking the skin there with his thumb repeatedly in a slow back-and-forth motion. I don't know what's taking him so long, but then I realize that, in his current condition, he probably isn't carrying oil.

I can rectify that. I close my eyes, concentrating for a moment, then move the bottle hidden under the mattress in our room to my hand out here.

"Here," I say, trying to pass the bottle to him. My hand is left hanging there, completely ignored. I frown. While Heath is definitely not his usual astute self under the moon, he's certainly been very sexually aware this entire time. He knows exactly how to play my body, how to make me come apart.

He certainly still knows he can't just slide into me without any preparation whatsoever.

His hands spread my ass so he can presumably stare at my hole, and then his warm, wet tongue is tracing my rim.

"Fuck." I drop the oil who-knows-where, not caring in the least as I slam my hand back to the ground for balance. At the same time, I'm tipping my hips up for a better angle, desperate for more of this.

There are no words, just want, a desperate, clawing sort of want, so strong that I think I might be the one overwhelmed with the magic of the moon.

Heath has his face buried in me like he wants to burrow inside, like he can't stand to be parted from me. He's making a mess of me, licking and sucking at me until I'm covered in his saliva, until it's dripping off of me.

"If you don't stop, you'll make me come," I warn him.

That does not seem to deter him at all. If anything, he becomes more desperate, holding my hips in place with a bruising grip.

My skin feels like it's on fire, like he's taken every inch of me and set me alight, like somehow, I could fly apart right now. I can barely think, and it's a chore to push past the haze of how good I feel.

And then he reaches forward and finds my cock, fisting it roughly, pushing me closer to the edge, not giving me a chance to hold on.

I fall, coming hard and messy, covering his hand in come. The orgasm is all-consuming, and my mind disconnects from my body for a moment. My arms collapse from under me.

When I muster the strength, I turn onto my back, lifting my head just enough to watch Heath.

He's licking his fingers clean. He's doing it slowly, too, watching me the entire time, and he knows exactly what he's doing. He might be half-feral right now, but he's more than aware of what he does to me, of how to make me crazy.

"As attractive as that is," I tell him, my voice sounding hoarse from the shouting I've probably been doing, "Wouldn't you rather fuck me?"

He better want to fuck me. I know he's particularly obsessed with taste and scent right this moment, but I need him inside me. I need him to want me like that, need him to satisfy me like that, and I think that he needs it too.

The two orgasms I've already had should have satiated me, but I feel like I'm starving for him, like I'll die if I don't get him inside me. Maybe the magic of the moon is working on me too, somehow.

Or maybe it's just my mate. Maybe I'm just desperate for him all the time, and it's unavoidable.

Will it ever go away? I know our mating bond is relatively new in the grand scheme of our lives. Perhaps this is a blush of infatuation, and perhaps it will fade.

He grabs my ankle and tugs me towards him, wrapping first one leg around his hips, then the other.

I squeeze him with my thighs, and all I can think is, gods, I hope it never fades.

He's still almost entirely dressed, and while he seemed unbothered by it earlier, now his trousers are annoying him. I barely resist laughing as he fumbles to lower them enough so he can fuck me like we both want.

I've lost track of the amount of times we've fucked in the past, but somehow it all feels new again. Like my body is more sensitive than it ever has been before, like Heath's deep, desperate thrusts are finding places inside me that I didn't even know existed. My cock hardens once more, desperately rallying as Heath pushes the two of us towards orgasm, his hand stroking my cock in time with his thrusts.

I grab his free hand off my hip, holding it in mine, needing something to squeeze as I lose control yet again.

Heath growls out my name as he comes, thrusting erratically inside me, spilling his seed in me as I squeeze around him.

He falls forward, pressing his face into my neck before he bites me deep enough to break skin. I yelp, but then he starts pressing mindless kisses to my chest and collarbone, and I don't resist, absolutely boneless underneath him while I try to catch my breath.

Eventually Heath starts to soften. When he at last slips out of me, he pulls back, and I see him eyeing my messy hole speculatively.

Oh, no. I can't allow that.

I use a bit of magic to move, deciding to re-write the rules of time and space for a brief moment until I'm right on top of him, sitting on his lap and pushing him back, sliding forward to straddle his stomach and pin his hands up to his head.

"I have never come so many times in a row in my life," I say, trying to sound stern, even as I know I just sound like a fucked-out mess. But I am a fucked-out mess, and we both know it. "And you need to give me a moment to recover before I collapse. So... it's your turn."

CHAPTER FORTY-THREE

HEATH

I wake up with Chase's head resting on my chest and a face full of his hair, complete with several leaves and twigs.

The sun is long since up, visible even over the top of the trees. I can't say I'm surprised; with how hard we went last night it's not a shock that both of us needed some extra rest.

Gods, that was...

For an unmated wolf, the full moon brings out a little more of our animalistic nature. We are a little wilder, a little less controlled, but I've been told over and over again that would be exponentially more as a mated wolf. I never knew quite how true that would be.

I struggle to sort through my memories, trying to determine if I remember every moment of last night or if there are missing pieces. If I did things I can't even remember. If I let go of control entirely.

If I hurt Chase.

I can't get a thorough look at him without moving him, and I don't want to upset his sleep. Still, at first glance, he seems all right to me. Surely he would not be sleeping so peacefully if I had turned into a wolf last night or hurt him in any way. I don't smell any blood, and his breathing sounds natural and pleasant. Surely, I didn't hurt him.

"You're thinking very hard," Chase murmurs, his breath tickling my chest as he speaks.

"How are you?" I ask, involuntarily tightening my hold on him.

He stretches against me, still without moving away from me. "I lost track of the times I came last night, and I'm not convinced that that wasn't its own energy draining form of magic, because I could sleep for another two days without any issue."

"Are you hurt? Did I take too much?" I ask, forcing myself to sit up so I can look him over the best I can.

He looks up at me from where he still lies on the ground. "I was fine until you took away my pillow," he mutters, and then, with seemingly great effort, drags himself so he can lie with his head in my lap.

I immediately move to run my hand through his hair, careful to avoid his horns. If I've worn him out as much as he says, then I don't want to accidentally start something again.

To tell the truth, I'm also more than a little worn out. It's a lazy, lethargic weight to my limbs, and my blood feels sluggish. I was too consumed by worry to realize, but I truly am exhausted.

Chase starts to trace a hand along my thigh by his head. "You need to relax, Heath. You're too hard on yourself. You're too worried that something is going to go wrong."

"Forgive me for being worried about the wolf," I say, trying my best not to snap at him. "We all know how close the wolf is to the surface with me, Chase."

He sighs and sits up, looking me in the eye. We're practically nose-to-nose, and all I can see is his dark eyes, determined and fierce.

"The wolf is close because you're creating your own danger, Heath," he says. "The wolf protected you, as it's meant to. You were in danger then. But now, worrying about the wolf, you're creating your own problems." He takes a deep breath. "Also, please stop acting like the wolf is the worst possible thing. The wolf is meant to protect you. That's all it wants."

I could say a thousand things to that. He's a demon, not a wolf, so he doesn't understand, not really. The wolf is never supposed to take control. The wolf is a constant presence, a set of instincts that rarely, if ever, steers us wrong, but I can count on one hand the number of wolves who have actually turned into their wolf forms. And blurring those boundaries between the pieces of myself seems to be something that can only lead to failure.

But the truth is... "It's not just the wolf," I admit.

Chase reaches for me, his hand slow so I could stop him if I wanted to, and traces the scar that bisects my eye now.

I flinch, but his finger doesn't lose contact with my face, a gentle but insistent touch.

The wound has healed into a scar, and I haven't yet worked up the courage to ask how bad it looks. I've thought, rather sourly, that ugly or clean, it would serve to distinguish Callum and I from each other. Bryce has always kept his hair shorter than we have, but the two of us have always looked nearly identical, and the scar would serve as a distinctive marker.

It was the only remotely positive outcome I could even think of. Everything else—the pain, the loss of vision, my inability to fight like I once did, the ugly reminder for anyone to see—weighs heavily on me.

But Chase doesn't touch it like it's an ugly wound. He touches me as gently as he always does. Reverently, even.

"I know," he says, voice barely a whisper. "But this isn't a problem, either."

I laugh brokenly. "I can't see right, I can't fight right..."

"You are six hundred years old," he interrupts me, voice firmer now. "Surely you've been inconvenienced before. And I'm not saying that this isn't a big inconvenience, but we already know you can work your way around it. You stripped the feared king of Demonheim of his legendary sword while the wound was still bleeding, with practically no vision. You can adjust."

"And if I can't?" I challenge, and I suppose I mean it to sound contrary, but I can't deny the little bit of desperation in my voice.

He removes his hand from my face. "You can. But if there's something you can't do, then that's an adjustment too. And I'll be here."

He stares at me for a long moment, as if willing me to get the message.

He's right is the thing. You can't live for centuries and not learn how to adjust to change. I lost my parents, saw my sister take the throne, saw the ensuing changes that were made to our pack. I watched my baby brother go from a scrapping child to a man who could beat me in nine fights out of ten.

This change affects me differently, I suppose, but not more or less. It just is. The curse of living forever, I suppose.

And then I think of Queen Olette, learning to live with the madness of the cages as well as the loss of her mate. I reach out and grab at Chase's hand, desperate for something to hold on to. As changes go, I'd rather lose both my eyes than my mate.

Chase seems to see my thoughts on my face, because he falls back to the moss beneath us with a dramatic sigh. "And now, you can hold me while I sleep for another six hours or so."

"We have a bed, you know." But I'm already laying down next to him, turning so I can bury my nose in the crook of his neck.

Gods, he smells delicious.

His hands find my hair. "My mistake. I'm sure both of us are ready to meet with your siblings right now."

I tense at even the idea of it, at the idea of my siblings around Chase right after I fucked him boneless under the full moon. "We need our own home."

It's not a new thought—no one who lived under the same roof as Celia and Bethany would fail to have thought of it—but it seems more urgent now than ever.

"If you want," he agrees.

A place of our own. A place to hold him like this, to be vulnerable together, to not have to worry about anyone else.

I love my siblings, and I would live and kill and die for them. I shared a womb with Bryce and Celia, shared everything I knew with Callum. But that doesn't mean that they are entitled to every part of me.

Chase's fingers scratch at my scalp. "Just sleep," he murmurs. "Worry later."

It's like all my worries, all my concerns, all the pressure of the last few weeks have been wrung out of me. There's nothing left, just me and Chase, exactly as it should be.

Chapter Forty-Four

Chase

When I wake up again, the sun is high in the sky, and Heath is kissing his way down my body.

I shiver under him, and he looks up. "Okay?"

I smile, watching his golden eyes, almost consumed entirely by pupil again despite the brightness of the sun. "If you think I can get it up again, then you're mistaken," I tell him. "Not even for you, Heath."

"Is that a challenge?" he asks, eyebrow raised, kissing along my stomach.

But my cock barely stirs.

Heath doesn't seem deterred, though, more focused on kissing and nuzzling my skin than attempting to actually arouse me.

And then my stomach growls.

He chuckles against my stomach. "I need to bring you home, hm?"

"Unless you plan to hunt and cook something fresh out here."

"You could cook too, you know."

"You made me come until I couldn't think. You owe me a meal."

"Oh, I do?"

"Yes," I decide, pulling slightly on his hair until he at last gives up and sits up.

"Where are our clothes?"

***

Once we finally find our clothing, we begin to walk back to the house. Inside, there's no evidence of Celia and Bethany, the two of them likely relaxing after the full moon as we should be.

Bryce and Callum are in the kitchen, though. Heath kisses the corner of my mouth softly. "Go relax," he murmurs. "I'll bring you food."

Well, I'm not going to argue. I go off to our bedroom, mentally daring either of Heath's brothers to make a comment about the limp I still have from last night. Thankfully, they don't say a word, letting me escape to our room in peace.

Heath enters a few minutes later, a plate of food in hand and a small smile present as he shuts the door behind him. "We're going to talk to Celia about building our own houses," he says.

"Right now?"

He snorts. "No one here is stupid enough to interrupt Celia the day after the full moon. Tomorrow, I suppose."

"They're that eager to get rid of us, hm?"

"Something about a few too many late-night noises." He sits on the edge of the bed, leaning closer to me to put the plate of food between us, offering bread and cheese and dried meat to me. Pickings apparently are lean when Bethany isn't ensuring we eat. "Want to build a home together, Chase?"

Hungry as I am, I ignore the food for the moment, pulling Heath further onto the bed so he's pressed against my side. "I can't think of anything better than that."

Celia looks contemplative when her brothers bring up the idea of new homes the next day.

"I know this place was mom and dad's, but, well..." Callum trails off, biting his lip as he looks at his sister.

She sighs. "But, it was for them and their children. Not for four new families after that. Alright. You're probably right." She gives Heath a sideways look. "You're loud, you know."

Heath squawks. "We're loud? I'm sorry, but who's spent the last several centuries screaming the roof down in this place?"

The table breaks into sibling bickering, each accusing the other of being more annoying, each finding reasons why they'd never want to live with any of the others again. And yet, somehow, I think they end up closer for it.

Not close enough they decide not to move out, fortunately. There're plans drawn for four new houses within the week. There's a brief argument for keeping the original house for one of them, but Bryce tentatively points out that it's drafty in the winters and the style is outdated and too big for any one sibling to take, anyway.

So the house is demolished, with planks from it—carefully, lovingly crafted by the four siblings' parents—laid into the four new houses, each rising in a line at the mouth of the valley.

Heath and I obsessively check over our plot of land, fretting over every detail of our new home. Heath's more invested than I am, although I'm more than a little eager at the thought of actually having a home, a place that is mine and his and ours. But Heath takes the obsession to a whole new level, dedicating every waking moment that he can spare to the work of building our house.

At no point does he seem to worry that he can't do it, or that he's in some way less capable now. If anything, the single-minded focus on the house seems to rejuvenate him.

The frame of the house is nearly done when Celia comes to us, arms crossed as she leans against a pile of lumber, watching us try to level a plank. "Don't you have magic, Chase?"

Honestly, I haven't even considered using magic for this. "I could try?"

"Don't you dare," Heath says. "We're making good enough progress as is." He looks up at his sister. "And you didn't come by to ask about magic."

"I'm here to steal your mate," she says unapologetically.

"Too bad, he's mine," Heath says, already looking back down at his work.

She rolls her eyes. "Part of being a pack is learning to share. I'm taking him now."

"What am I supposed to do without him?" Heath challenges. "This work requires two people."

"Don't worry. You'll be busy yourself soon. Callum was looking for you."

Not seeing a way out of it, I follow after Celia.

***

Celia's new house isn't any more complete than ours, so her office is currently in tatters. Instead, she talks with me while she walks, a large, looping circle around the village.

"I need you to be our intermediary with the demons," she says.

"That's what Bryce does," I protest, nearly missing a step to think of me somehow being given Bryce's role in the pack.

"And Bryce absolutely agrees that, in this case, you'll be more effective than he will be," she continues. "You know them, the new king and queen."

"Not well," I say automatically, evidently determined to argue as much as possible today.

"I don't think you could argue that one of us knows them better."

"Heath seems to actually know Hannah."

"Heath is busy. Callum isn't going to let him out of training. Besides—Heath can do many things, and I appreciate him for all of them. I still think it's better to send a demon to form an alliance with demons."

"And is that what you're after? An alliance?"

"You're pack now, Chase," she says, and I have to pretend that I don't nearly trip over my own feet when I hear that. She keeps walking like she doesn't notice, although I'm convinced Celia notices just about everything that happens in this village. "And that makes them, by extension, pack. Trust me when I say that wolves take that seriously. And I need to ensure that your king understands that."

My mouth goes dry, and I have no idea what to say. Celia acts like this is perfectly natural, and continues walking at the same, steady pace.

Finally, I say, "I'll go. When?"

She hands me a folded piece of paper. "Whenever you're ready."

CHAPTER FORTY-FIVE

HEATH

"Go away, Callum," I say, not turning to look at my little brother. It's harder to finish this work without Chase, but not impossible.

The plank slips from my hand, too bulky and awkward to balance it properly on my own. "Fuck. Or come help."

"Take a break," Callum suggests, not even twitching a finger to help.

"I'm busy."

"What are you going to get done without Chase, exactly?" Something pokes me in the back, and I hope it's not the tip of a sword. "I thought happily mated bliss was all about working together. Not doing anything alone."

Whatever it is pokes me a little harder. It definitely is a sword. "What do you want?"

"You're slacking on training again."

"I'm not one of your soldiers," I tell him, finally conceding to turn around and acknowledge him.

He shrugs. "No, you're Celia's soldier. And you need to be ready if she needs you. Are you ready right now?"

"Fuck off, Callum."

He clicks his tongue like he's actually scolding me. "Rude. Tell you what. Give me half an hour. That's it."

"I don't have to give you anything." That might not strictly be true, I suppose. Callum's right about me being Celia's soldier, because we all are. It doesn't mean I can't make this difficult for Callum, though.

"Listen, I heard you beat the shit out of the former king of Demonheim still bleeding from that eye. Whatever's going on with the eye now, surely you can at least duplicate that."

He holds out the sword insistently, and I know my brother. He'll wait all day. Callum's been a stubborn ass since he was a toddler, and time hasn't improved him in the slightest.

"Half an hour," I say grudgingly, taking the sword.

"Half an hour," he agrees. He draws his own sword. "Now, are you going to get out of there, or do we risk knocking your house over?"

We walk to the training grounds, and I'm relieved that at least no one else is here today. I can be spared that humiliation, at least.

Callum, being Callum, doesn't start with nice words. He doesn't make sure I'm ready, not even in consideration of my poor vision. Instead, he turns, takes a fighting stance, and swings.

And it's all I can do to dodge.

He immediately puts me on the defensive, pushing me further and further back until I'm almost at the edge of the marked training field. I try turning directions, but he's always there, ready to redirect my path, pushing me exactly where he wants me.

Gods, is my brother frustrating. I half regret every moment I ever put into teaching him.

I'm a moment too slow to process all his strikes, always a fraction off at predicting where they'll land, and every second costs me, allowing Callum to control the fight almost entirely.

"You're better than this, Heath," he says, just loud enough to be heard after he nearly trips me.

I snarl. "You think some things might have changed?"

He shrugs, a movement so casual it's absolutely galling when paired with a powerful follow-up jab. "So, how'd you do it in Demonheim?"

Sheer, terrified desperation and the need to protect my mate. Neither of which I'll ever achieve knowing my brother is my opponent. Asshole as he is sometimes, I couldn't ever convince myself that he'd actually hurt me.

But there's more to it than just that, I realize. Yes, I'd been terrified, and I'd been desperate. But I'd also been clever. And I'd done it by being a wolf. By relying on sound, and smell, and the way the air feels when it moves. By ignoring my sight when it confused me or complicated the situation.

I close my eyes, plant my feet, and feel the moment Callum begins his next strike.

My block is unerringly placed, and I brace myself for the hard hit. It lands exactly as it should, right where I'd want it to for maximum effectiveness. Now, I'm in the perfect position to strike back.

And it works.

I turn the tides of the fight, working my way out of the corner Callum backed us into, and steer the fight where I want it. Callum matches me blow for blow, his strikes fast and powerful, but at least he's not pushing me around anymore.

At last, clapping pierces the air. I know it's Celia before I even open my eyes, her scent mingling with our sweat.

"Truce," Callum says, noticing her too, and we drop our blades. I'm gratified to find him breathing heavily, at least.

"I see we're back in form," Celia says to me.

"Seems like it." I don't want to talk about it, not yet—maybe not ever. But she's not wrong.

"You should know your mate is gone," she says, and before I can panic, she adds, "He went to deliver a message to the demons for me."

I raise an eyebrow. "Putting him to work?"

"We all pull our weight around here," she says, sounding like our father for just a moment. "And I'm very interested to see what kind of weight the two of you can pull together now, with you back. His magic is quite interesting. Disappearing and reappearing... lots of possibilities."

"Don't exhaust him."

She snorts. "Like you'd ever let me. He told me to tell you to call him back tonight. He said to give him a few hours, and then you can bring him back?"

"I can," I confirm.

"Great," Callum says. "Are we done here?"

I cross my arms. "You came to get me, so you tell me."

He sheaths his sword and clasps me on the shoulder. "I think I got what I came for. But we're not done. Tomorrow?"

And, strangely, I think I'm looking forward to it.

***

Distracting myself without Chase is nearly torture. We haven't been apart for more than a few hours since the cages, and those are memories I'd prefer not to revisit anytime soon.

The house keeps me busy, at least. I'd like to have a place for my mate and I to live, and soon. We need a place just for us, somewhere we can really call home.

When the sun begins to set, though, I'm getting itchy to have him home. It's selfish, but I don't like the idea of him spending too long in Demonheim, a place I can't follow.

I honestly don't care if he's in the middle of a sentence with King Ryder right at this moment. Celia said I should call home in the evening, and I'm more than ready to have him home.

"Chase."

Nothing happens. Perhaps the distance being greater means it will take a little longer. I wait, mostly patiently, eager to have him back in my arms.

"Chase." Nothing. "Chase. Chase. Chase. Chase." I start saying his name so rapidly, words tripping over each other, desperately begging for this to work.

Nothing.

I don't understand. The name is a contract, he's told me that. It had worked in battle. It had worked in the cages. I know we're in different realms, faced with great distance, but there is no reason why it shouldn't work today.

The sound coming out of me is now more a desperate complaint than his name, but I can't help it. I can't think straight, my blood pumping like I'm in battle. My mate. My mate is missing from my side, and I can't get to him.

My mind goes directly to the worst possible situations. Is he in the cages? He's appeared and disappeared from there before, but it drained most of his energy. Would I be able to summon him out?

I won't take no for an answer, I decide immediately. I will find my way back to Demonheim, banging down the walls that separate the realms, and find Chase. I will fight my way through if I need to.

***

Just my luck, Celia is with Callum and Bryce, leaving me having to confront all my siblings, even while I look crazed. I can't help it. Then again, I challenge any wolf to not look deranged if their mate is trapped in a different realm.

I barely get out my explanation of Chase's disappearance. I keep tripping over my word, and I doubt they understand my hurried attempts to explain the magic.

Bryce raises an eyebrow. "Negotiations can take time, Heath."

"He wouldn't ignore me calling. He doesn't ignore me calling. Something's happened."

"Give him some time," Callum suggests.

I ignore both Callum and Bryce. It's not their fault; they haven't found their mates yet. They don't know what I'm going through, how it feels.

So I turn to Celia, the only one here who will understand me. "I'm going to get my mate," I tell her, forcing my voice to be steadier, begging her to believe that I'm rational. "And you can either help me, or not. I'm still going for him."

Celia just stares back, but at last she nods. Then she motions to Callum. "Get him a weapon. And go with him, I suppose. I'd like Heath not to get involved in two wars in Demonheim in one year."

I don't know if Callum would stop me. Frankly, he's liable to jump into the fight by my side. So, I don't protest. Maybe he's exactly what I need.

Maybe Celia knows that, too, because she nods at me.

Callum sighs. "How do we find Demonheim?"

I know where Ryder's war camp was, and I have to consider that as a start. And if there's not an obvious way to enter Demonheim from there, I will make one. I will tear down the walls between worlds if I need to.

Nothing will keep me from Chase.

Callum gives me a sword, then raises an eyebrow. "We're walking?"

"Unless you know magic, yes."

He doesn't argue. We're both used to walking anyway, and it's always better if you just get started.

CHAPTER FORTY-SIX

CHASE

Demonheim is disappointing, frankly.

I never expected to feel that. When I thought of Demonheim since I left, I'd remembered it with some level of fondness. It had been my home for centuries, after all.

And I suppose all of that is still true, but there's no pang of nostalgia, no desire to call this home again.

If anything, I miss the house Heath and I are building. Even in the early stages of building like it is now, it feels more like home than Demonheim does.

It is nice to see Ryder and Hannah, and see what changes they've already brought to Demonheim. The realm even looks better, my father's obsession with the human image of hell erased as the halls turn back to the clean, elegant stone fortress Demonheim used to be. Demons mingle around, and I see many faces that I know were refugees in the crowd.

Ryder and Hannah have abandoned their rather ornate thrones to sit in a more modest office. They welcome me in with genuine grace and take

Celia's note gratefully. I read Celia's note over Ryder's shoulder, unable to help it.

To King Ryder, the rightful ruler of Demonheim:

To my knowledge, demons and wolves have never had a recognized alliance, beyond the understanding of us all regarding the purposes of the cages. Perhaps you and I can be the ones to change that.

I believe a stronger alliance could benefit us both. But more than that, you're pack now; any family of Chase's is family of mine, too. Chase will always be your subject, but he is just as much a Crae now as he is yours.

My heart swells, and my throat tightens. Celia goes on to list all the things she'd expect from an ally and all the things she'd offer in turn, but I can hardly pay attention, too struck by the simple declaration that I am one of theirs now.

Hannah looks at me, eyes soft, her hand on her mate's shoulder, and I know she understands too. There's something magical when someone purposefully carves out a place for you.

Ryder reads slowly, carefully, despite the letter not being long or complicated. Maybe he's looking for hidden meaning, or maybe he's just exercising the cautiousness of a king.

Then he writes out his own reply, taking far too long. I start shifting from foot to foot, unable to help it.

Heath should call me home soon. Celia said she'd have him call me in the evening, and while time has less meaning in this realm, I know enough time has passed that it has to be evening now.

Ryder hands me the note, carefully folded, and smiles wryly at me. "So, you're liking it with them, hm?"

I swallow, trying to think of how to say it without insulting what he offered me before I left. But I won't lie, and he doesn't look upset. "We're building a house."

"That's great," Hannah says. "Keep him from doing anything stupid, huh? I've heard about that man running headfirst into too many stupid things."

Ryder just shrugs. "Him running headfirst into stupid things is what brought him to Demonheim."

True enough. Still, I agree more with Hannah, even if I can't even bear to think of Heath and I not meeting.

We would have met eventually, of that I'm sure. There is no force in the universe that could tear us apart.

Speaking of, I should be back at his side any moment now. The mating bond feels like a cord stretched too tight between us, and I need to be back with him.

But as we continue chatting, the call never comes.

Hannah realizes first. "When did you tell him to call you?"

"His sister said she'd tell him," I mumble. If it were anyone else, I might think Celia did it on purpose. But she's too organized to forget, and after what she wrote about me in her letter, I can't think she'd purposefully leave me stranded.

Ryder seems to have caught on, a worried frown creasing his brow. "That's a long distance," he murmurs. "A lot of energy without him calling you. You can stay here."

I shrug. "I brought him and your mother out of the cages and survived it just fine. I can survive this."

There are a thousand reasons why he might not have called me yet, I remind myself. Surely, nothing is wrong.

Ryder stands, clasping my shoulder. "You'll be back?"

I nod to where Celia's letter is still on his desk. "Apparently, it's now an official role."

"You can come whether it's official or not."

I manage a smile, reaching up to squeeze his forearm. "I know." And I do, too. Somehow, I, Chase the unwanted, have gone from barely fitting in Demonheim to having two homes, both of which genuinely want me.

Well, I thought they did, at least.

Chapter Forty-Seven

Heath

Callum and I are only an hour or so from the village when Chase appears in front of me, falling directly into my arms.

I instinctively grab him tight, which is good, because he immediately sags, unable to support his own weight.

"Whoa! Chase? Chase, sweetheart?" I demand, squeezing at him and locking my knees so we don't both fall over.

He groans. "What the fuck?"

"What did they do to you?" I demand, and I know my fingers are biting into his skin as I squeeze him, but I can't help it. I feel like I almost lost him, like we've crossed oceans to be here together at this moment.

Did he come from the cages after all? Is that why he's worn down like this?

"What did they do?" he asks, and I think he's aiming for indignation, but his voice is unsteady and weak. "You—"

He doesn't say anymore, passing out right into my arms.

Callum swears, moving to steady me as I shift under Chase's weight. "Well, let's get him home," he says, turning sharply on one heel.

I shift so I can carry Chase in my arms, turning so I can bring him back to the village and figure out what the hell happened.

After a while, Callum clears his throat. "I can carry him."

"No." It comes out too sharp, so I swallow, trying to moderate my tone. "When he wears himself out like this, energy from me helps. I'll hold him. It'll help him recover faster."

Callum shrugs. "Whatever you say. Any idea when he'll wake?"

I have no idea, and it's physically painful. I don't know how to wake him, how to help him. I remember how long he slept after the cages, and just hope this will be easier.

He starts stirring when we've crested the mountain, the village in view again. I go to my knees, cradling him, not wanting him to wake up while we're moving and jostling around.

"Heath?" he asks, eyes still closed.

"That's me," I promise, tracing his face with the tips of my fingers. "What happened, Chase? What did they do?"

"You said that before." His voice is soft, like he's speaking from another room. "They didn't do anything. You didn't call me."

"I absolutely fucking did call you. Probably two dozen times."

"He called you," Callum confirms over my shoulder, not even pretending not to listen in. "You should have seen his panic."

Chase tries to push himself up so he can sit, so I move him until he's sitting on my lap, holding him to me. Seemingly without thought, his hands gravitate to my arms, holding on tight.

"Then why didn't it work?" he demands. "The contract worked in the cages. There's no reason it shouldn't work now."

"If we try it, will it knock you out again?" Callum asks.

"Heath needs to call me. Not you," Chase replies firmly.

I look down at where he's grabbing me. "Have to let me go, sweetheart."

It takes a moment, but he does, so I carefully slide him onto the ground, moving an arm's length away.

"Chase." Nothing, again, and my panic is only soothed by being able to see him. "Why the hell doesn't it work anymore?"

"I don't know," he snaps, frustration clear in his voice, his brow furrowed as he thinks. "There's nothing special about it; the demon's name acts as the contract, and..." He trails off. "What if that's not my name?"

"What are you talking about? You're Chase. Who else would you possibly be?" I demand.

Bizarrely, he flushes, turning his eyes away. "Your sister had me bring a letter to Ryder," he mutters. "She called me a Crae."

Something tender and gentle blossoms in my chest, taking up every inch of space there. I move closer until I can grip his chin and tilt his face back to mine. "Do you want to be a Crae, sweetheart?"

"I want a family," he says. "If you want me."

"I want you forever," I promise. I reluctantly drop my hold on his face, then slide just far enough back that I can't touch him anymore. "Chase Crae," I say, and before I can blink, he's in my arms, pushing me back so I'm lying in the cool grass, his weight on top of me, pinning me to the ground.

I never want to be anywhere else.

EPILOGUE: CHASE

PRESENT DAY

"You ready yet?"

"Almost," Heath says, strapping his sword belt on.

"You think you need a sword belt to go to Demonheim?"

"That's only our first stop," he points out. "Besides, after what happened to Marielle and Callum—I'm ready for anything."

He means it, too. Heath is braced for anything and everything to come our way.

Considering what happened, it's a sound strategy. I just don't think he needs it in Demonheim, because my brother's court has never been anything but hospitable to us, even after all these centuries.

I don't consider Demonheim my home, and I never will again. Our house is right here, the one we've built and rebuilt with our own hands. But I like to know that I can go back, sometimes.

Of course, this isn't a pleasure trip. This will be me calling in on the alliance Ryder made with Celia, asking the demons to support us against the group looking to chop halflings up into parts.

Considering Hannah's also a halfling, something tells me this will be an easy sell.

Which is why Celia has only sent us there as a first step. After that, we're to do what we do best.

As she's always said, Heath is very good at being places he shouldn't be. And my magic means all doors are open when I want them to be.

Apparently ready to go, he pulls me into a kiss, long and sloppy and a little desperate. I groan, immediately kissing him back, grabbing him by the waist to hold him tighter to me.

"What was that?" I ask when he finally pulls away.

"Call it for luck, or for energy, or just because I love kissing you," he says, proving his point by kissing along my jaw. "Call it whatever you want."

Ryder is expecting us by this point, most likely. And we have a war to plan and a war to win.

I pull him into another kiss, hands desperate in his hair, and he grabs me tighter in response.

Just another minute.

LOOKING FOR MORE?

Receive a special bonus short story about the start of Ryder and Hannah's love story if you sign up for my newsletter at www.addyjameswriter.com!

ALSO BY ADDISON JAMES

Crae Romance

Callum

Bryce

Heath

Celia

Silas

Estrid

Supernatural Christmas

A Werewolf for Christmas

A Recipe for Love

Standalones

The Heat Cure

Dragon's Treasure

About the Author

Addison James is a romance book author from New England. They are obsessed with all things mythical, mystical, and magical. A lifelong fantasy reader, that evolved to fantasy romance as they grew up. Addison always has a story to tell and is excited to introduce you to their world of fantasy and paranormal romance.

You can find Addison at addyjameswriter.com or at addyjames@addy-jameswriter.com.

www.ingramcontent.com/pod-product-compliance
Lightning Source LLC
Chambersburg PA
CBHW020720130726
47899CB00011B/584